Sudden

Clarence Budington Kelland

Alpha Editions

This edition published in 2024

ISBN : 9789364730358

Design and Setting By
Alpha Editions
www.alphaedis.com
Email - info@alphaedis.com

As per information held with us this book is in Public Domain.
This book is a reproduction of an important historical work. Alpha Editions uses the best technology to reproduce historical work in the same manner it was first published to preserve its original nature. Any marks or number seen are left intentionally to preserve its true form.

Contents

CHAPTER I .... - 1 -

CHAPTER II .... - 6 -

CHAPTER III .... - 14 -

CHAPTER IV .... - 21 -

CHAPTER V .... - 27 -

CHAPTER VI .... - 32 -

CHAPTER VII .... - 38 -

CHAPTER VIII .... - 44 -

CHAPTER IX .... - 51 -

CHAPTER X .... - 57 -

CHAPTER XI .... - 64 -

CHAPTER XII .... - 70 -

CHAPTER XIII .... - 78 -

CHAPTER XIV .... - 86 -

CHAPTER XV .... - 93 -

CHAPTER XVI .... - 99 -

CHAPTER XVII	- 106 -
CHAPTER XVIII	- 112 -
CHAPTER XIX	- 116 -
CHAPTER XX	- 123 -
CHAPTER XXI	- 127 -
CHAPTER XXII	- 136 -
CHAPTER XXIII	- 142 -
CHAPTER XXIV	- 149 -
CHAPTER XXV	- 155 -

CHAPTER I

It is not a fact that clothespins are threshed out like beans or wheat. They are not a product of nature, but of art and machinery. A clear understanding of this is necessary before the story can begin to march; for if clothespins had grown in fields inclosed by rail fences, and were gathered by the aid of a self-binder, there never would have been an individual known from coast to coast as Clothespin Jimmy. This individual would not have had a son named James, nor would Clothespin Jimmy have started to build a new clothespin-mill in Diversity, Michigan. So it is manifest that the fact stated in the first paragraph hereof lies at the very tap-root of the whole matter.

If you studied sufficiently over the hieroglyphics appended by Clothespin Jimmy at the end of a check you discovered them to indicate the signature "James Ashe." But it required more than a passing glance. Nobody ever quarreled with the signature, because it suited the old man and was honored by the bank.

The owner of the illegible signature was sixty-five years old, was hale, hearty, and ripe for adventure. Also he figured that fifty years of hard labor about completed his sentence and that he was entitled to play about.

Therefore he called home his son James, who had shown an early and marked distaste for the clothespin business, and took him into the library, where there lived in ease and idleness some ninety feet of assorted red, blue and black books. He opened the conversation:

"Son, what name do folks call you by when they speak to you?"

"Why—Jim, I guess."

"Just Jim? Nothing describin' it?"

"That's all."

"Why?"

"I haven't the least notion, father. Why should they call me anything else?"

"No reason in the world. That's what I'm gettin' at in my feeble way. What do folks call me?"

"Clothespin Jimmy," replied his son, promptly.

"Yes, and when I die that's what's goin' onto the headstone. It means somethin'. There hain't no need for a verse of poetry and clasped hands. 'Clothespin Jimmy' tells the whole story. I don't mind sayin' I'm proud of it. Just like I was proud of the first dollar I ever handled—because I earned it. Folks call me Clothespin Jimmy because I've done things with clothespins—things that amount to somethin'. Men don't git names like that by settin' in one spot till their pants wear thin. Now, take you—they call you Jim, and there the matter ends. That's where you end. You're just Jim, like seven hundred thousand other Jims. You don't stick up above the herd. Hain't it about time folks was findin' reason to hitch a descriptive name onto you?"

"I'm twenty-eight. I've got a good job. I'm supporting myself and not taking a cent from you—"

"I'm not findin' fault with what you've done, son. You ain't a gilded butterfly—that ain't what I mean. You're respectable and self-supportin', but so's twenty million other boys in this country. You're just a good average human critter. But that's not even comin' close to the subject, which is that ma and me would like to go to Californy."

"Good idea, dad. When do you start?"

"As things is we don't start at all."

"Why?"

"Largely because you're satisfied to have folks call you Jim without any description to it." The old gentleman took a package of folded papers from a drawer and slid the rubber band off them.

"Here's somethin'," he said. "Bonds. Fifty of 'em for a thousand dollars apiece. Net five per cent. I've milked the business to get 'em. 'Twasn't right by the business, but I done it just the same. Now, then, you never liked the clothespin business. Don't know why. So I've fixed it so you could pick and choose between two things. I'll come to that in a minute. But first, about Californy. I started supportin' myself when I was fifteen, and I've been hard at it ever since—fifty years. The time's come for me to git out with your ma and have a good time if we're ever a-goin' to. Short time for frolickin' left at best. But it rests with you. I figger I've earned the right to loaf, but I can't loaf without leavin' somebody to labor. There hain't nobody but you." He stopped and looked at Jim and slapped the package of bonds on the desk-top three or four times.

"There ought to be somethin' to you more 'n just Jim. I've waited to see it crop out. Now I'm goin' to dig for it. Here's these bonds. Yonder in Diversity is the new mill almost ready to start turnin' over. It'll be worth a quarter of a million to somebody. I can make it so in a year. What I got you in here for was to offer you your choice. You can take the mill and the business and have it till God does you part—and buckle in like I've done;

or you can take this fifty thousand in bonds and go play. If you take the mill, your ma and me take the bonds and go play. There's the proposition. Take which you like—and no hard feelin's."

"But, dad, suppose I don't take either?"

The old man's face changed; his eyes grew anxious; the hand that held the bonds trembled ever so little.

"You wouldn't do that to me, son. Ever since that night twenty-eight years ago when I heard a miserable squawkin' sound up-stairs and mistrusted it was you, I've been workin' and plannin' and hopin'—with you as the object of it all. I wanted to fix things for you, son—and I've done it. You don't need to take the business if you don't want to. Your ma and me can keep on like we've been goin', and have consid'able fun, too. But if you was to refuse both, then I'd feel as if I'd sort of wasted my time—as if my workin' and livin' hadn't been for no good at all. You—you wouldn't do that to your dad, would you, son?"

Young Jim walked to the window and stood looking out, and as he looked out he reviewed his own plans and scheme of life, his hopes and private aspirations. Presently he turned:

"No, dad, I won't refuse both. I'll take one or the other."

Clothespin Jimmy's face showed his relief.

"Much 'bliged, son," he said, as though he were accepting a notable favor instead of giving away what folks not addicted to polo or divorces or Fifth Avenue or ocean-going yachts would consider a fortune.

Jim returned to his window; his father sat thumbing the bonds and waiting. Presently the old man spoke suddenly:

"I don't want you tradin' unsight-unseen. You're entitled to know what you're up against. In case you take the mill—I milked it for these bonds. I told you that. The business will need this money and need it bad. I've built big. The day the mill starts runnin' you h'ist a debt of seventy thousand dollars onto your shoulder. You'll be pinched for money, and you'll have a devil of a time. But I could pull it through—and so can you if you're any good. You ain't steppin' into a snap—not by several statute miles. Furthermore, if you take her you take her for better or for worse. You git no help from me. These bonds'll be all I have, and I'll need 'em. I won't let loose of one of 'em to keep you out of bankruptcy. Understand?"

"Yes," said Jim.

"Got your mind made up?"

"I'd rather sleep on it, dad. Suppose we put it off till to-morrow."

"If you're the man to handle the job you can decide now. Puttin' off never helped matters. A man that makes up his mind right off may be wrong half the time, but he's right a whole lot more than the fellow who has to have a decision jerked out of him with an ox-team. If you expect to get anywheres in this world, learn to make up your mind swift and follow up with swift action. We'll finish the deal now before quittin'-time."

Jim turned and looked at his father. Somehow he felt detached from himself, as if he were sitting at a distance twiddling his thumbs and watching his own wheels go round. He occupied the position of spectator very briefly, however, but popped back inside of himself and took possession again—with a noticeable change. He felt different. He did not feel like Jim Ashe as he had been acquainted with Jim Ashe, but like another individual of markedly different characteristics. This change manifested itself in his reply:

"All right. We'll decide now. Now!"

"Yes?" said Clothespin Jimmy, his fingers tightening ever so little.

"I take the mill," said Jim.

"Huh!" his father said.

That was all. He slipped the bonds into his side pocket. From another pocket he drew an envelope holding two long, many-times-folded strips of blue paper. Jim recognized them as railroad tickets.

"You'd better go to Diversity on Friday. This is Tuesday. Your ma and me leave for Californy on Friday mornin'."

Jim eyed his father suspiciously. "Had the tickets all the time?"

"Yes."

"You were going, anyhow?"

"No; not unless you took the mill." The old man chuckled.

Jim snorted. "Pretty sure how I'd decide, weren't you?"

"Well, seein' as you're my son—and your ma's—I wasn't more 'n a mite worried. I figgered you was sound timber, but there was always the chance that sap rot had got at you. That envelope there was the stock certificates, all indorsed over to you, inside of it. Take 'em. You're the proprietor of the Ashe Clothespin Company now. I'm through with it. Fifty years of work to earn a couple of years of play for ma and me. When we're gone write us often. We'll need to hear from you. But don't you dast to mention clothespins to me—either good or bad about 'em. I'm through. Through for good and all—and it's up to you."

"Done." said young James.

CHAPTER II

Young Jim Ashe rode from five o'clock in the morning until two in the afternoon on a train that carried him through a stretch of the State of Michigan that not even a local poet had ventured to call lovely. It was flat as an exhausted purse—indeed, it was an exhausted purse, for its wealth in straight, clean pine had long since poured from it, down its rivers to mills where it had been minted into money. With this money a second generation that did not know a wanigan from a cook-shanty, cork pine from Norway, nor the difference between the Doyle and Scribner scales, was getting its names in the Sunday papers and illustrated magazines as bold and hardy owners of imported Chow dogs.

At the end of nine hours of travel through the sort of scenery that would make the decorations of a modern New York hotel a restful diversion, Jim thought even a game of coon can with a traveling-man which, as everybody knows, is the world's most futile method of passing time—would be a boon from heaven. But there was neither drummer nor cards. He was not the sort of person who could sit and think, and when tired of that omit the thinking and just sit. So he brooded. Long before he reached Diversity he was terribly sorry for himself, which, after all, is a species of mild pleasure enjoyed by many. One conclusion he did reach—namely, that Diversity must be the ultimate fag-end of desolation trimmed with a fringe of black despair. When the train stopped at Diversity's depot he looked out and felt that conclusion to be sound.

The first thing he saw was heat. He could see it rising in little wiggling waves from the blackened sand; he could see it at work raising more blisters on the paint of the station; he could see it struggling in vain to reduce the weight of the baggage-master, who was also telegraph-operator, station-agent, porter, and information bureau. The next thing he saw was a jumble of form and color that would have made immortal a cubist who could have caught it and labeled it "A Hole Raveled in Civilization's Heel." But if the cubist had caught it he probably would have called it "Gentleman in Union Suit Climbing a Telegraph Pole," and so passed Fame by on the other side.

The station reminded him for all the world of a flabby, disreputable redbird, squatting in the midst of an hilariously ragamuffin brood which sat back on its tails and derided her scurrilously. The progeny consisted of coal-sheds, warehouses, nondescript buildings where nothing was or apparently ever had been done, a feed-mill and a water-tank. All of them seemed to detest the perpendicular; most of them leered through doors squeezed to the shape of a clumsy diamond. Fire, thought Jim, would bring a merciful release to the whole of them.

He alighted with all the pleasant anticipation of a Christian martyr about to dip into a caldron of boiling oil. No one was there to meet him, for no one knew he was coming. He didn't know where to go and didn't much care. All directions seemed equally unpromising. However, before plunging into the unknown he stopped in the shade of the building, mopped his forehead, and took an observation.

Standing with the sun beating down upon her was a young woman who looked at the departing train with an expression like one Jim had seen on a girl's face as she stood in the bread-line. It spoke hunger. In spite of his own discomfort Jim was interested, and there can be no doubt he stared. He stared long enough to observe that the young woman was dark, with a heap of curling hair so black that even the old, hard-working simile of the raven's wing was not of the slightest use to him. She was small, but had one of those exquisite figures which just a little startle one.

She did not impress Jim as at all pretty, but she did impress him as a young person who might find difficulty in letting somebody else have his own way.

She continued to stare hungrily after the train, but presently she turned her eyes so they met Jim's stare. In a second she comprehended he was staring, and she flashed resentment at him. She even bit her lip with vexation. Then she turned abruptly—but very gracefully, Jim noticed—and walked across the tracks.

Jim flushed uncomfortably and looked about to see if anybody had noticed his bit of bad manners and its result. In a ramshackle buggy drawn up to the platform sat an old man with square white whiskers. Possibly "sat" is not the precise word to use, for the old man rested mainly on the back of his neck, allowing the rest of his body to clutter up the space intended only for his legs and feet. Jim picked up his bag and approached.

"Could you drive me to the hotel?" he asked.

The old man looked at Jim's feet, at his ankles, his knees, his belt-buckle, his cravat, finally into his eyes. This took time, and the sun was hot on Jim's head.

"I could," said the old man, finally. Then he wiggled the lines. "Giddap, Tiffany," he said, wholly oblivious to Jim's presence on earth. "Giddap there. Stir yourself. G'long."

Jim stood goggling after him, as nonplussed as if the old fellow had suddenly developed the old-fashioned dragon habit of spouting smoke and flames. Behind Jim the fat station-agent laughed twice, thus: "Heh! Heh!" which was all he could manage on account of his weight and the heat. Jim's ears burned; he snatched up his grip and followed in the wake of the buggy.

He halted before a sign which proclaimed that here was the Diversity House. There did not seem to be a great deal of bustle connected with this establishment; as a matter of fact, there was no sign of life at all unless you count an unshaven gentleman in white woolen socks and a calico shirt, who lent the support of his back to a post on the piazza and snored feebly. Jim went in. The office was deserted. He coughed. In another month Jim knew how useless it was to seek to attract attention in that hotel by coughing, indeed by anything short of exploding dynamite on the floor. Next he tried kicking the counter. At best it was only a hollow-sounding sort of kick and got no results whatever. Jim was growing impatient, so he inserted three or four fingers in his mouth and whistled. It was a lovely, ear-splitting, sleep-piercing whistle, and Jim heard a movement on the porch.

The gentleman of the white socks peered through the window, feeling of his ear as though it had been sorely abused, and looked at Jim disapprovingly.

"Gosh all hemlock!" exclaimed the gentleman, mildly.

"Are you the proprietor?" Jim demanded.

The gentleman stared some more. "Who? Me? Ho! Don't calc'late to be," he said.

"Where is he? Dead?"

"If he is he hain't let on to nobody. Seems though he might be over t' the printin'-office playin' cribbage."

"What do I do? Wait till he comes back before I get a room?"

"Hain't no objections, but mostly they go up and pick out the room they like."

Jim sighed impatiently and placed his bag on the counter.

"Can you tell me where the new mill is being built?"

"Down the road a piece. Keep right a-goin' and you can't miss the dum thing."

"Thank you," said Jim, and started out to inspect the plant of which he had become proprietor.

Jim walked down the street, which did not run ahead in a straight line, but meandered about aimlessly as though trying for all it was worth to keep under the shade of the fine big maples which bordered it. Nobody could blame it. In fact, Jim thought it showed extraordinary intelligence for an illiterate, unpaved, country clodhopper of a road, for the shade was the pleasantest, most friendly thing he had found in Diversity.

In five minutes he rounded a bend and came upon a flat which seemed like a huge platter on which somebody was trying to fry a number of large and small buildings. Half an eye could tell the buildings were new, indeed unfinished. Heat-waves radiated from their composition roofs, and as for their corrugated-iron sides, Jim fancied their ugly red was not due so much to paint as to the fact that they were red-hot. Everywhere were men hurrying about as if it were a reasonable day and they weren't in the least danger of sunstroke. Inside Jim could hear the clang of hammers, the rasp of saws, the multitude of sounds which denote the business of an army of workmen.

It looked very big and raw and uninviting to him. There was nothing homey about it at all. It didn't even look interesting, and Jim stood under a tree and wished his father had chosen some other calling than the manufacture of clothespins. He mopped his head and wrinkled his nose, and grew very gloomy at the thought that down there on that unspeakable flat lay the work of his future years. His dreams had been of something very different.

He shrugged his shoulders and walked rapidly down on to his property, acting very much like a man with a tender tooth on his way to the dentist's.

As he walked along the side of the biggest building he encountered a small Italian boy with a big pail of water.

"Son," he said, "where's the office? Where's the boss?"

The big black eyes lighted; white teeth gleamed.

"You lika drink? Sure. I take you da office."

Jim drank and followed the boy, whose bare feet seemed miraculously to take no harm from the rubbish he walked over.

"Me Pete." he said, pointing to himself. "Me carry da drink." Then he pointed to a small frame shack. "Dat da office," he said.

Jim walked through the half-open door. Nobody was there. On a drafting-table were drawings and blue-prints; a roll-top desk was littered with papers and letters. Jim sat down in a revolving-chair to wait for the return of Mr. Wattrous, the engineer in charge of construction. It was very hot and stuffy, so he removed hat and coat and made himself at home.

A man with a red face, a wilted collar, and a leather document case entered presently.

"Afternoon," he said, sinking into a chair and mopping his face. "White's my name. Fire-proof paint. Jenkins was sick, so I came up, but I guess you and me can fix things as well as him, eh?"

Before Jim could reply the individual continued: "Now we can't afford to pay you any fifteen per cent. commission out of our own pockets. 'Tain't right we should. But here's what we will do: We'll stand seven and a half and we'll just add seven and a half to the face of the invoices. See? You'll get your fifteen all right and we won't get stung for but half of it. Neat scheme and fair to all sides, eh?"

"Does sound neat," Jim said, "but not economical."

Mr. White laughed, as at a witticism.

"You poor engineers has got to live," he said.

"True. Just out of curiosity, what price would you be making us if there weren't any commissions to pay?"

"Umm, well—I guess we could figure twenty per cent. off what it's going to cost you."

Jim said nothing, but scratched his head. He wondered if Wattrous had added twenty per cent. to costs all the way through. If so he had not been a profitable investment.

"You'll O. K. the invoices?"

"I guess likely I will—hereafter," said Jim, and turned to observe a heavy-set man in corduroys and laced boots who entered with a roll of drawings in his hands. This person looked inquiringly from Jim to White.

"Make yourselves at home," he said, ironically.

"Much obliged," said Jim, feeling now for the first time a real interest in life. Indeed, he felt a sort of humorous interest. The situation was not without its ludicrous appeal. "Mr. Wattrous," he said, "allow me to present Mr. White. Mr. White sells fire-proof paint."

Wattrous scowled, seemed a bit perplexed. As for White, his jaw dropped and he stared at Jim and then at Wattrous with the expression of a man who has been violently struck in the wind.

"Yes," said Jim, "Mr. White is generous. The way he hands out commissions would astonish you. Why, he's going to give you fifteen per cent. just for buying paint from him."

Wattrous thrust out his jaw. "Who the devil are you?" he said.

"Ashe," said Jim; "James Ashe. I'm the fellow that owns this mill."

Mr. White made an unsuccessful attempt to rise, but fell back under Wattrous's furious glance; he tried again, more successfully, and scuttled out of the office at a speed that threatened further to wreck his already lamentably wilted collar. Jim turned sharply to Wattrous. He felt unlike himself; felt the urge of a will he had not before experienced; felt a sense of confidence; felt, indeed, a desire to do something and to do it without delay.

"You, Wattrous—of course you're fired." His voice hardened, became peremptory without his volition. It seemed to do so of its own accord, and Jim was conscious of mild surprise at it. "Get off the job, and get quick," he said, "before I decide to pitch you off."

Wattrous was of two minds. The first was to bulldoze this young man and see if he couldn't roar his way out of his unpleasant predicament; the other was to make matters worse by the application of personal violence. He would have admired to thrash Jim. Jim read his mind and pointed to the door.

"Git," he said.

Wattrous hesitated an instant, then swung on his heel and strode away muttering.

"I hope he meets up with White," Jim said to himself with a grin. "Nobody'll get hurt who doesn't deserve it." Then he leaned back in his chair and gazed at the ceiling, reviewing the last few moments. He had made a new acquaintance—the acquaintance of Jim Ashe functioning in an emergency—and it was a surprise to him.

"Is that the kind of man I am?" he asked himself.

Well, here he was. He was on the job, in the very midst of it, a quite different beginning from what he anticipated. He had expected to merge quietly into the affairs of his new property, but he had not merged into it unless one can say that a hammer thrown through a glass window merges into it. He had expected to enter his work with repugnance; now he looked forward to his next official act with a tingle of pleasant anticipation. After all, there might be more to business than he suspected.

"What next?" he asked himself. He had, so to speak, cut off the hand that directed, the head that planned. They must be replaced, and Jim himself had not the technical knowledge to fill the lack. He went to the door and looked out; there, grinning up at him, was little Pete, pail in hand.

"Hello, Misser Boss!" said the boy.

"I take it you've been here right along," said Jim, good-naturedly.

"All da time. I hear you fire Misser Wattrous. Whee!"

"I take it I have your approval."

"Uh-huh," said Pete, clearly not at all understanding what approval was. "I tell Italian mans. Dey laugh. You real boss. Speakaqueek—bang! Italian mans lika dat."

"Fine. Now, Pete, who's the next boss—who else besides Mr. Wattrous?"

"Oh, Misser Nelson. He boss. Work wit' da hammer and saw, too."

"Nelson, to be sure." Nelson, Jim remembered, was the head millwright in the old plant. "Where is he, Pete?"

"I show. You come."

Pete led the way. As they neared the main building a young man not older than Jim emerged from the door. His overalls were covered with grease and sawdust, a rule protruded from a narrow pocket; quite evidently he was of the carpentering clan.

"Dat Misser Nelson," yelled Pete.

"Oh, Nelson!" called Jim.

The young man paused and turned a handsome, sharply cut face toward Jim. It was a dependable face, a likable face, a face, if the steel-blue eyes were to be believed, which belonged to a man whose action would follow swiftly his words, or even precede them. He did not reply to Jim's hail, but stood waiting.

"Nelson," said Jim, "my name is Ashe. My father has gone to California and I am in charge here."

He paused briefly, and Nelson extended his hand with a suddenly brightening smile.

"Glad to know you, Mr. Ashe."

"I've just fired Wattrous. Somebody's got to take charge in his place. Can you take hold and make this mill run?"

"Yes."

"Good! You're boss. What are we paying you?"

"Four dollars a day."

"Wages. Your salary will be thirty-five dollars a week. When can we begin to turn over?"

"Mr. Wattrous figured four weeks."

"We'll start to manufacture in three. Put on more men if necessary. Now let's see where we're at."

Nelson showed Jim through the mill, explaining what must be done here, what was lacking there, why this machine sat so, why another machine must be driven from counter-shafting. He told him about the conveyer system, about everything, for mills and machinery were alike strange and mysterious to Jim.

"Is the general plan good?"

"Yes. But if it were my mill I would—"

"It is your mill. Make it run and make it run right. I'm going back to the office to have a look-see at the books and files."

As he sat in the revolving-chair he felt again a wave of astonishment at himself. Was this Jim Ashe—the same Jim Ashe who got off the train at Diversity an hour ago? Most certainly it was, and yet how little that Jim Ashe knew about himself.

"I guess I'm due for a personal inventory," he said to himself.

He was aroused from his investigations by the whistle of the hoisting-engine. It was six o'clock. He put on his coat and walked toward the road, and as he went workmen nodded and smiled to him.

"The old man's son," he heard as he passed.

"Nelson says he's hell on wheels," was another scrap of comment; but the one that pleased him most, because it was unexpected, because it would have pleased most his father, was spoken from the opposite side of the fence out of his view:

"I heard him talkin' to Nelson. He'll make things hum."

"Who will?" asked another voice, apparently joining the group.

"Why, Sudden Jim—Clothespin Jimmy's boy."

Jim walked back to the hotel with a new buoyancy in his heart; his first half-day had been good. It had introduced him to himself—and it had won him a name.

CHAPTER III

Supper at the Diversity House surprised Jim Ashe so much that it almost ruined his appetite. He had expected the food to match the general efficiency of the place, and had vaguely figured on the possibility of dining on crackers and cheese. This teaches us that, whereas man judges from the outward appearance, he should wait till he sees what comes out of the kitchen. It was the sort of meal you might expect to eat in a prosperous farm-house—plentiful, well cooked, and topped by apple pie that made Jim wish he had started with dessert, continued with dessert, and ended up with a final helping of it. There are few things in this world more delightful than a splendid meal that takes you by surprise.

He went out to sit on the porch, cool now with the evening breeze off Lake Michigan. Sitting with his back against a post, and looking as if he had not shifted his position since Jim saw him early in the afternoon, was the gentleman of the white socks and calico shirt. He did not look up as Jim passed to take a chair at the end of the piazza.

Presently there drew up before the hotel a ramshackle buggy drawn by an animal that was undoubtedly still a horse. It was a very Methuselah among horses. The old man who rode in the buggy appeared comparatively youthful beside it. Jim smiled at the turnout, then frowned a trifle, for the old man was the same individual who had rebuffed him so bruskly at the depot.

"Hey!" called the old gentleman, without straightening himself from the amazing position in which he sat. "Hey, Dolf—Dolf Springer!"

"Eh?" the gentleman in the white socks grunted, sitting erect and gazing about him owlishly.

"Was you at the depot to see the six-o'clock come in, Dolf? Eh?"

"Calc'lated to be."

"Anybody git off, Dolf? Anybody special?"

"Lafe Jenks and his wife, Mandy Williams, Tom Sweet, two travelin'-men—"

"Anybody special, Dolf? Eh?"

"Well, last to git down was Michael Moran, Judge."

"Um! What become of him, Dolf? Happen to notice?"

"In there eatin' his supper."

"Calc'late to be here long, Dolf?"

"Quite a spell, Judge."

"Calc'late to be here till Moran comes out?"

"I could."

"Um! Figger on speakin' to him, Dolf?"

"Did think I might."

"What was you goin' to speak about? The weather? Eh?"

"Not's I know of, Judge."

"Was you goin' to mention me? Eh? Figger on alludin' to me?"

"Thought some of it."

"As how, Dolf?"

"Thought I might mention you was askin' after him."

"Um! Goin' to tell him where I was headin' for? Eh? Think of doin' that?"

"Figgered I'd mention you was to your office."

"G'-by, Dolf."

"G'-by, Judge."

The old man clucked to his horse: "Giddap, Tiffany! G'long there! Time's passin' rapid for both of us. Don't waste none of it. G'long!" The equipage drew slowly away from the hotel and proceeded down the street at a rate of speed which came close to being no movement at all, until it came to a halt again before a frame building at the end of the block. Here the old man alighted, hitched his horse as carefully as if the animal were a two-year-old showing signs of a desire to bolt. Then he went inside.

In ten minutes a man of middle age, not at all the Diversity type of citizen, appeared in the doorway. He was below medium height, sturdily built, with a face of the aggressive-business-man variety. Dolf Springer uncoiled by a mighty effort and rose to his feet.

"Howdy, Mr. Moran!" he said.

Mr. Moran nodded curtly.

"Zaanan's to his office. He wants to see you over there."

Mr. Moran nodded again and walked briskly down the street to the building before which stood the ancient horse and vehicle. He had wasted no time obeying the summons, and Jim wondered somewhat, for Michael Moran did not appear to him a man who was accustomed to run about at the beck and call of old men in dilapidated buggies. He seemed rather a person used to issuing orders and to exacting prompt obedience.

He was curious, too, about the old man himself, who, without uttering a word that could be construed by a court of law as expressing his wishes in the matter, had, nevertheless, directed Dolf Springer to waylay Mr. Moran and give him a message. The old man's method was a splendid example of caution. It delighted Jim and aroused his curiosity as to the name and place in the world of the old fellow.

He made inquiries of a fellow-lounger on the piazza:

"Who is the old gentleman who drives a horse named Tiffany—"

"Who? Hain't been in Diversity township much, have you? Guess not. That there's Zaanan Frame, justice of the peace. Been it nigh to thirty year, and like to be it thirty year more."

This was meager enough information, but Jim's informant seemed to think it ample, for he relapsed into somnolent silence.

Jim was just rising with the intention of taking a walk—that seeming to be the sole entertainment offered by Diversity—when another buggy, dust-covered, drawn by a team, stopped before the hotel, and a small, wiry, exceedingly well-tailored old gentleman, with white whiskers of the bank-president type, alighted. He got down jauntily, springily, pertly, and trotted up the steps.

"Mr. Ashe—Mr. James Ashe, Junior. Can anybody direct me to him?"

"I am Mr. Ashe," said Jim, stepping forward.

"Delighted to meet you, young man." The dapper little gentleman stood off at arm's-length to appraise him. "Don't favor your daddy much. Foot longer and two feet narrower." He chuckled gaily. "My name's Welliver—Morton J. Welliver. Bet you've heard of me, eh? Bet you've heard daddy mention me once or twice."

"Of course. Your name, with Mr. Jenkins's and Mr. Plum's and Mr. Mannikin's, is pretty average familiar to me. I hope everything is satisfactory at your plant."

"Satisfactory? My boy, the Brockville Hardwood Company is booming. Now's the day for the clothespin man. We're at the top of the heap. Prices up, competition down, market hungry. But what's this I hear about daddy?

Wired him I wanted to see him on clothespin business. He wired back: 'Out of the game. Son owns plant—lock, stock, and barrel. Tell it to him.' Now, what's that mean?"

"Just what it says, I expect. Father has gone to California with mother. The plant's mine."

"Clothespin Jimmy quit! Can't believe it. Thought he'd die with one foot on a maple log and a clothespin in each hand. Well! Well! So you and I have to talk business, eh?"

"If there's any to talk," said Jim.

"I reckon there's some—some. Where'll we go to do it?"

"We might walk out a piece and sit on a fence," said Jim, with a grin. "It'll be more comfortable, and we can argue and swing our arms better."

"Good enough. Which way?"

They walked along, Welliver doing most of the conversing. Indeed, it was Mr. Welliver's habit to do most of the conversing. He owned a great many words and was willing to part with them freely—but not unwisely. It was said by men in the business that Mr. Welliver could keep you entertained for an evening and not utter a word of what was on his mind. Clothespin Jimmy once told him he was like the what-d'ye-call-'em fish that squirted out a cloud of ink and then hid in it.

"Guess we can stop here," said Jim when they arrived at a spot overlooking the flat on which the new mills were rising. "That's the plant below."

"Um! Some bigger than the old one, eh? What's the idea? Going to take all the business away from us old fellows?"

"I guess you and Mr. Jenkins and Mr. Plum and Mr. Mannikin can look after your share, if all I've heard is true."

"We can try. We can try. And that, my boy, is the very reason I'm here. I'm told you're putting in six more clothespin machines than you had in the old plant."

Jim nodded.

"That means about one hundred and twenty-five thousand additional five-gross boxes going on to the market."

"So father says."

"Well, son, the Club don't look on that with a favorable eye. Of course you know the Club?"

"Clothespin Club? I know we're members of it with seven other mills."

"But do you know what it has done for the business? How it has taken a scramble of unprofitable competition and turned it into a smooth-running machine?"

"Something about it."

"The Club meets—socially, of course, and nothing to interest the Sherman Law fellows. But we sort of talk things over friendly, and somebody quotes a price on clothespins, and another fellow says that sounds like a fair price, and they talk over market conditions and go home. But they all stick to the price mentioned. The last price was up-top, and we're all making hay. But we don't want anything to disturb the market."

"Um!" said Jim, who was beginning to glean a hint of Mr. Welliver's object.

"Conditions are about right now. Any increase in output will—unsettle matters."

Jim remained silent.

"So," said Mr. Welliver in his most friendly way, "the Club had a little meeting—"

"Part of it," interjected Jim.

"All but you," said Mr. Welliver. "Yes, we met casually, and talked it over, and here I am to advise you against adding those extra machines."

"You're a bit late," said Jim. "They're added."

"But you might find it more profitable not to operate them. More money can be made with twelve machines at present prices than with eighteen and four or five tens lopped off."

"Very possibly."

"Well?"

Jim understood then. Mr. Welliver's last observation had not been an observation at all—it had been a threat.

"You mean you'll cut prices if I go ahead?" He paused a moment. "You got together and decided the Ashe Clothespin Company had bitten off all it could chew, and this was a good time to sort of help us run our business, eh?"

"We know how much you've put into these mills. We know your daddy built them on the strength of high prices, and we know that a drop in prices will give you something to think about."

"And your ultimatum is: Either we drop our six new machines or you drop prices. Is that the idea?"

"Something very like it."

Jim got to his feet and stood over the dapper little man. He looked large in the moonlight and Mr. Welliver became uneasy in his mind. He contemplated with negligible pleasure the idea of this big young man's losing his temper and rumpling him all up. But Jim had no such idea.

"Mr. Welliver," he said, "father gave me this business and told me to run it. He didn't tell me to let the Club run it—and I'm not going to. You've come here threatening me, and somehow I don't take to the idea of it. I know where I'm at and pretty much what I'm up against, but just the same I'm the Ashe Clothespin Company, and I'll keep on being it as long as there's a company. I'll run twelve machines or eighteen or fifty, as I think it's wise, and if the Club doesn't like it, why the Club can be just as peevish as it wants to. I've never been in a good fight yet. You seem to want to get into one, and I'll accommodate you for all I've got. Now, then, here's my proposition to the Club: It can go on and run its own affairs and leave me alone—or it can start a row. You can make your choice now. What is it?"

"We can't allow you to run those extra machines."

"It's war, then?"

"I hope not that, but we'll have to point out to you that one mill can't upset the whole industry."

"And I'll point out to you that this mill can do as it everlastingly pleases. Let's go back to the hotel. Is it shake hands or fight?"

"I'm afraid it'll have to be fight."

"Then," Jim said—and all of a sudden he felt grimly glad, and a grimly glad smile lighted his face "then I guess I'll fire the first shot. Our inventory shows we've got fifty thousand boxes in the old warehouse. They go on the market to-morrow at five tens off the present price—and if that doesn't suit you I'll cut off another ten or so."

"But—but, my boy, you're crazy. You'll lose money on every box you sell."

"So will you—and you've got more to sell than I have just now. You can watch me send the telegram," Jim said.

"Young man, you're a bit sudden," said Mr. Welliver.

"I may be sudden, sir, but you'll find I'm lasting, too. When this ruction calms down one of two things will have happened: I'll be busted or the Club will have learned to stick to the purpose for which it was formed."

He turned and strode off toward the hotel, with Mr. Welliver trotting at his heels, uttering bleating sounds of protest. As they neared the piazza, he said, pantingly: "Suppose we talk some more. Maybe we can hit on a compromise."

"The only compromise you can hit on is to keep your hands off."

Mr. Welliver shrugged his shoulders.

"Good night, young man. I'm afraid you're going to be very sorry for this. Your father had more—discretion."

"My father's backbone reached from the base of his skull to the seat of his pants," said Jim, "and every inch of it was stiff. Good night, Mr. Welliver."

Inside he procured a telegraph blank and wrote a brief message to the bookkeeper at the old office:

> Notify all agents and customers price clothespins five tens off list. Effective to-day.

Again something to do had arisen and Jim had done it swiftly, suddenly. He had added fresh and stronger claims on his new name.

CHAPTER IV

Jim awoke next morning to a sense not altogether one of satisfaction with the events of the night before. He realized he had inaugurated a clothespin war which further parleying might have postponed or prevented. Again he had acted swiftly, suddenly, surprisingly to himself. Yet as he thought it over he was less inclined to censure himself. He felt he was right when he insisted on building and operating his mill to suit himself—so long as he built and operated with fairness. He knew Welliver and the Club would not recede from their position, and that there remained only to surrender, play for delay, or fight. There is a certain satisfaction in striking first.

Jim's watch told him it would not be six o'clock for another half-hour, and breakfast was not until seven. He dressed leisurely and descended to the piazza, where, grouped about the step of the buggy, stood Welliver, Michael Moran, and the old justice of the peace.

"Good morning," called Welliver, chipper as a wren. "You're an early bird. Thought I'd have to leave without saying good-by."

"Hope you have a pleasant drive," said Jim. He turned down the walk and strode away with the intention of tramping a mile or two before the dining-room opened.

"Wait a minute, son," Welliver called. "Come here and shake hands with Mr. Moran—you'll be meeting each other in a business way considerable. He owns this thirty-mile streak of rust you call a railroad. And Judge Frame."

Jim shook hands. Moran returned his pressure heartily; but, while he offered a cordial welcome to Diversity, Jim was aware the man's clear gray eyes were studying and appraising him. As for Zaanan Frame, he merely grunted.

"Haven't had a change of heart since last night?" asked Welliver.

Jim smiled and shook his head. "Our folks will be quoting a discount of five tens this morning," Be said.

"Son, when you've been in this business twenty years you'll go slower."

"Colts," said Zaanan Frame, "kicks out the dashboard jest for fun. But most gen'ally, when an old hoss starts in to use his heels he means business."

James said nothing. He was to discover that Zaanan Frame was given to making remarks to which it was difficult to retort; that Zaanan had a way of dropping a statement over a conversation as one would lower a candle-snuffer over the flame, and that a new subject to talk about became immediately desirable. The old justice was a final sort of person. Jim's dislike for him grew like one of these huge white mushrooms which daring individuals pick and fry and eat—and sometimes survive.

"You are determined?" asked Mr. Welliver, making one last effort.

"I'm determined to run my own business," said Jim.

Mr. Welliver shrugged his erect and beautifully tailored shoulders.

"When you've got enough—" he began, suggestively, but did not trouble to finish the sentence.

"Glad to have met you, gentlemen," Jim said. "I'm off for a walk to stir up enthusiasm for breakfast."

A man who has to have his clothes wet through before he can recognize it is raining may succeed as a professor of Greek or as an artificer of a ditch, but he is not likely to elbow aside numerous captains of industry. Though unequipped with that which the proverb declares to be the best teacher, Jim Ashe did have in its proper place inside his skull a brain reasonably able to travel from patent cause to obvious effect, or to reach a conclusion that birds which flock together are likely to be similarly feathered. The height of stupidity for a man in Jim's situation would have been not to speculate on the manifest acquaintance between Mr. Welliver, Michael Moran, and Justice of the Peace Frame. He was not guilty of that stupidity, and as he walked along the road whose hot sands had cooled under the summer moon, he speculated on the significance of their early morning meeting. His thoughts ran something to the effect that to a man up a tree it looked as if Mr. Welliver had allies in the very heart of the territory of the Ashe Clothespin Company.

Jim walked briskly past his mills, then turned into an inviting lane which led upward toward a wood-lot. Presently he turned again, to return cross-lots along the hypotenuse of the triangle. To do this it was necessary to surmount the first line of defense, a five-strand, barb-wire fence, then to climb a knoll surmounted by a lonely hickory-tree. From the top of this knoll Jim hoped to have a general view of the country and so to acquaint himself at a glance with the topography of his new home. He scrambled up, and reached the top breathless. The last dozen feet had been steep, hiding the tiny plateau at the peak from sight. Immediately he straightened up. He was made to feel that he was not wholly welcome—indeed, that he was decidedly an intruder, for frowning at him with black brows and sullen black eyes was the young woman at whom he had stared on the station platform.

Her expression was hostile. If eyes and compressed lips can speak, that young woman was saying peremptorily and not at all politely, "Get out!"

"I beg your pardon," Jim panted. "I had no idea—?"

"You must have seen me," she said, coldly.

"But I didn't see you," said Jim. "I should not have intruded."

"This spot is visible for a mile in any direction," she said, shortly. Apparently she was determined to believe he had seen her and had climbed up to her, probably in the prosecution of the common masculine ambition to scrape up acquaintance with a stray and unprotected girl. Jim felt an embarrassing warmth about his ears.

"You stared at me yesterday," she said, before he could speak.

"I did not stare at you," he replied, unguardedly. "I was staring at the expression in your eyes—the hungry expression with which you looked after the train."

She bit her lips; her eyes darkened; she was startled.

"Can people see it?" she asked, aloud, not of Jim, not of herself, not of anybody or anything that could frame an answer.

Jim ignored her exclamation and entered his defense. "I was walking to pass the time till breakfast. When I got to the wood-lot there I turned to cut across lots. I did not see you. I had other things on my mind than unexpected young women on hilltops at unholy hours in the morning. I am sorry I disturbed you." He did not go, but stood looking down at her. She was looking past him down the valley toward the distant shimmer that was the great lake. For the moment he was negligible to her; again her eyes, her face, wore that expression as of the woman in the bread-line—of hunger.

In a moment her face relaxed till it spoke merely of discontent, dissatisfaction. Jim thought she would have been homely were it not for the graceful setting of her head on her shoulders, the splendid ease and symmetry of her position.

"I don't have to explain to every chance stranger why I get up early in the morning and come here," she said, not so much sullenly as with repression, as though she were damming up something within her.

"Of course not," said Jim, inadequately.

Suddenly she flashed to her feet with a beautiful litheness and stood facing him, her hands clenched into little fists, her breast heaving.

"I will tell you. I've got to tell somebody. It's because I hate this"—she swept her hand over Diversity. "It's because it's horrible, unbearable. It's because I'm chained down here like a prisoner in a dungeon. That's why I go to watch the train—it is going away, going out there where people live. That's why I come up here. It's my little window to look out of. I can see beyond Diversity. Sometimes a vessel passes. I imagine I am on it, going away—to Chicago—to New York—to San Francisco. Here I can turn my back on Diversity and see where its dead hand cannot reach. I hate the town, I hate the people, but most of all I hate the children. Oh, look shocked! But sit in a room with thirty of them ten months a year; watch their smugness; try to cram spelling and geography and arithmetic into them; try to make an impression on their dullness. They're a nightmare! That's why I come here—to look away from them, beyond them, to see a spot that's not tainted with them. I was born here." She said the last as though it were the summing up of all evil.

"My dear young lady," said Jim, in a tone that was ludicrously paternal, "you're working yourself up to—hysterics or something."

She leaned against the old hickory-tree, panting, clutching the folds of her skirt with convulsive fingers.

"I want to go—go—go! I want to see things—to be a part of them. I'm smothered. This is living in a graveyard where there's a perpetual fog. Other people live. Other people have things happen to them, and I—I don't even dare read about them in books. I couldn't stand it."

Jim wanted to run, yet he wanted to stay. Here was a manifestation far outside the purview of his experience. It was a little adventure into a human soul, and Jim's contact with the human soul had been superficial.

"If you want to go, why—why in thunder don't you go?" he said, boyishly.

She flashed a gleam of scorn upon him. "I'm a girl—a girl—the most helpless, most defenseless, most easily damaged thing under the sun. Why don't I go?" Her tone snapped with scorn. "What would I do? Who would take me in? What would become of me? Here I'm safe. I may die of it, but I'm safe. It might be less hideously barren if I weren't. I'm alone. I've been alone since I was fifteen. Some day it'll be too much for me and I'll go. But I won't be fooled into it. I'll go with my eyes open, knowing why I go. If I go nobody'll be to blame—except Diversity—for I'll have made my choice deliberately. Don't look shocked. I suppose there have been millions of others before me who had the same choice to make. I'm not unique. You men have made the world, and when you get a glimpse of it once in a while you're shocked."

"Miss"—Jim paused and bit his finger in bewilderment—"I don't just know what you're accusing us men of, nor the world in general. But I've lived a bit more than you. I've lived enough to know this—that there's more good than evil. There are more folks who are trying to do right than who deliberately do wrong. I know that even in the bad ones there's more good than bad. I believe if you were to take all the law and machinery of the law, all the police, all the social protection out of the world to-day, that to-morrow the force for right which is in the world would assert itself. There is so much more good than bad in the world that the bad would be held down by the mere weight of the good. You hear about the evil, because the evil thing is news, something to talk about, something to make readers for the newspapers. And it's news because it's out of the normal. So there seems to be a lot more bad than there is. Goodness is normal—so normal that nobody notices it."

"Men always defend themselves plausibly."

"I'm not defending men; I'm defending humanity."

She fell silent, and gazed past him again to the twinkling blue of the lake. When she spoke it was less hardily, more wistfully than she had spoken before:

"The world is so big and so interesting. In any direction, if my eyes reached far enough, they would see something thrilling. To think there is so much—and I am refused a crumb!"

"I'm afraid something has happened to disturb you."

She laughed shortly. "If something should I'd thank Heaven for it! It's all so drowsy, so placid, and I'm tied to it as if to a stake, with a slow fire lighted round me."

"But if you want to go so badly, if life here is so unendurable, what ties you to it?"

"The trifling accident of having been born a girl, added to the trifling episode of having lost my parents, added to the inconsequential condition that the forty dollars a month I get for teaching school is all that stands between me and starvation."

She turned abruptly from him and started down the knoll. He followed.

"Don't come with me," she said, stopping. "I don't know you. I don't want to know you. After this I never want to see you again. I had to say these things to somebody. By accident it was you, but I hate you for it. You know. Never try to speak to me."

She went away swiftly, leaving him to stare after her in bewilderment. He was startled. His sensation was such as if he had picked up a pebble and found it suddenly to be a live coal.

Later in the day he found her name to be Marie Ducharme, daughter of a French-Canadian lumber-lack who had risen to be a walking boss. He found that Diversity returned her dislike, or, if it did not return it, viewed her askance as a person who was "queer."

To be "queer" in a village of less than a thousand souls is no inconsiderable crime.

CHAPTER V

For the next fortnight Jim Ashe was too busy to give thought to his new environment, to study the new world to which he had been translated. He was studying the clothespin business. It is true he did not come to his work wholly unprepared; being Clothespin Jimmy's son, that was impossible. His father had talked it, thought it, dreamed it. Jim had assimilated it with his meals. Also, as a boy, before his college days, in vacation times when college days arrived, he had worked in the mills and acquired for the business that distaste which he once vainly fancied was to lead him down widely different vocational paths.

As a lad he had counted and packed pins; later he had dogged in the sawmill; one vacation he had calloused and slivered his hands feeding the drum. He had scaled timber; he had been chore-boy for old Pazzy Miller, the pinmaker. These various jobs were given him out of his father's wisdom to show him the how and the why of all steps in the manufacture. Nor was he ignorant of other branches of the business, for clothespins were not the sole product, though they were its backbone. He was not unacquainted with the mysteries of the veneer lathe nor with the making of wood ashes. He understood somewhat the technic of the turner, and the processes which went to the making of wooden spoons, rolling-pins, drumsticks, and the like—all turned from seasoned lumber.

Those things he knew as a workman. Something of the marketing problems his father had been able to drop unsuspected into his mind, but this was all incoherent, not card-indexed and pigeonholed and ready for instant use. Jim spent his time—not occupied by immediately pressing concerns and events—in preparing the knowledge he had, in adding to it; in short, in preparing himself as best he could to handle and husband the property that was his. It was surprisingly like trying to swim after a course of twenty lessons from a correspondence school.

A week before the machinery was ready to turn over, the office force with its paraphernalia arrived from the old office and was installed in the new. It consisted of one stenographer, picked by Clothespin Jimmy wholly for efficiency and not at all for adornment; of a middle-aged bookkeeper, who seemed to have been born with something more than the normal quantity of organs, for there grew from his forehead a green eye-shade, without which he was never seen, and there sprouted in his right hand a pen. There was also an assistant bookkeeper, whose business in life was to act and look as much like the bookkeeper, Mr. Grierson, as possible; and a shipping-clerk, whose familiarity with freight-rates and with the occult business of routing freight-cars so they would arrive where they were intended to go, instead of at the other side of the continent, was such as to arouse Jim's admiration.

The clothespin war was as yet a minor trouble. He had one letter from the secretary of the Club, informing him that the price he had quoted was cut by another five per cent. This cut he met immediately. A flood of orders came in from brokers, traveling-men, wholesalers—all rushing to take advantage of the low market to stock up. These Jim culled over carefully, accepting only enough to keep his plant running to capacity, not overloading himself with orders which he would have to fill in case of a cessation of hostilities and consequent soaring of price.

He called into conference his superintendent, millwright, master mechanic, and the foremen of his departments, but it was not a conference, as the event proved. It consisted merely of a brief statement by Jim.

"The job you fellows are up against," he said, "is to manufacture better and cheaper than anybody else. Prices are down. I believe we can still show a profit. Any man who has an idea that will save a tenth of a cent on a box of pins will find it profitable to bring it to me. What's the best day's average you made in the old plant, Pete?"

"Seventy-five boxes a machine," said the old pinmaker.

"I'm expecting eighty here," Jim told him. "It costs as much to operate a machine making sixty boxes as it does eighty. If you can make eighty, the extra five will come close to being profit. Don't let a machine, a lathe, a saw, waste machine hours. Everything has got to run; it has got to run constantly, and it has got to produce the greatest quantity that is physically possible. I'm depending on you men. We have a new crew in large part. I want them to feel I'm depending on them. Tell every girl, every man of the crew, that the Ashe Clothespin Company is depending on her or on him, and that each may depend on me. If I expect them to give me a square deal, I expect myself to give them a square deal. Tell them that. There'll be no dissatisfaction or labor trouble here if I can help it—and I can. I guess that's all. Now get at it."

The men looked at one another; old Pete scratched his head and grinned, and they filed out. Their feeling, if one was to judge from their faces, was one of satisfaction and confidence. They believed in the new boss, and that is the first step toward a feeling of affection.

It was that afternoon that Zaanan Frame drove his old horse Tiffany—named, as Jim found out, after the greatest of legal books, Tiffany's *Justices' Guide*—up to the mill and rheumatically climbed to the office.

"Afternoon," said he. "Name's Jim, hain't it?"

Jim nodded curtly. He suspected the justice of being no friend of his, but an ally of the other camp.

"All right, Jim. Last names was made for fellers that git to be postmasters. Couldn't sort the mail without 'em. Hain't for every-day use no more 'n plug hats."

"What can I do for you, Judge?" Jim asked, offishly.

The old fellow regarded him a moment in silence.

"Wa-al, you might put more sugar into your coffee. Need sweet'nin' up. Still livin' to the hotel, eh? All the comforts of home? Suits you to a tee?"

"The meals are all right," said Jim, unbending a trifle, "but that's all you can say."

"Um! What's home without a motto over the door? Hain't met Mis' Stickney? Course not. Widder woman twice repeated. Machinery runnin'? Um! Got her goin' quicker 'n folks expected."

"We hurried things up a bit."

"To be sure. Never seen sich a woman as the Widder Stickney for house-cleanin'. Best housekeeper in the county. Mill makes a heap of difference in Diversity. Kind of irritatin' to Lafe Meggs up to the store. Says somebody's always comin' in and disturbin' him to buy somethin' or other. Calc'lates he'll have to hire a clerk. Lafe's ambitions mostly requires a sittin' posture."

"How big is this town, Judge?"

"About a dozen people and five hundred folks. Take in the newspaper, Jim?"

"I take a Grand Rapids paper."

"Take in the Diversity paper, Jim?"

"No."

"Um! Comes out Thursdays. Int'restin' readin' into it sometimes. The Widder Stickney got her second husband on the strength of her cookin'. Calc'late she could git a third with it, but she allows husbands is so fleetin' and funeral expenses is so high 'twouldn't hardly pay. Name of the paper is the *Diversity Eagle*. Business perty good, eh? Keepin' up brisk?"

"We manage to keep from loafing."

"To be sure. Loafin's the leadin' sport here. Calc'late Dolf Springer's our champion jest now. Interestin' piece in the paper this week. Several interestin' pieces. Don't take it in, eh? Early riser, hain't you? See you walkin' 'fore breakfast."

Jim wondered if the old justice had any ulterior meaning in this observation. He had arisen early each morning and tramped out into the country. Sometimes he had been close to admitting to himself that this was not wholly for the air and exercise. Indeed, he had wondered if something much more material and human had not been at the root of the matter. There, for instance, was that young woman whom he had encountered on top of the knoll. She walked of mornings, too—and she was an interesting if not attractive individual. She puzzled him. He even went so far as to be vaguely anxious about her, for her state of mind had not appealed to him as one conducive to normal and conventional behavior. He wondered if Zaanan Frame knew of that encounter, or knew of that subsequent meeting—and passing—a week later when Miss Ducharme had come face to face with him at a turn of the road and had gone by with nothing to indicate she was aware of his existence except a scornful flash of her black eyes.

"Somebody was sayin'," he heard Zaanan observe, "that the Widder Stickney had a spare room she was thinkin' of rentin'. Yes, sir, if I was goin' to read the *Diversity Eagle* I figger this week's issue'd be the one I'd look for. Um! Calc'late Tiffany's tired of standin'. Have to humor him. Powerful high-spirited boss. Second-floor room on the front, it was. G'-by, Jim. *Eagle* office is next to Lafe Meggs's store."

The old man went out, and it seemed as if he creaked in every joint. Jim heard him pass slowly along the hall and out of the door—and wondered what his visit meant. He reviewed the rambling conversation as best he could; found that in spite of himself he was attracted by Zaanan's personality. But why had the old fellow come? What had he talked about? Why, about the Widow Stickney and her room, and about the *Diversity Eagle*. Jim was not yet familiar with Zaanan Frame's methods, but it did seem clear to him that the old justice wanted him to go to board with Mrs. Stickney; wanted him also to read the current issue of the *Eagle*.

That evening Jim procured a copy of the *Eagle*. Its leading article gave the news that Michael Moran had purchased a controlling interest in the Diversity Hardwood Company, and had been elected its president in the place of Henry W. Green, resigned. This was worth while. It was important, for the prosperity of the Ashe Clothespin Company depended on the Diversity Hardwood Company. It was the latter that furnished the birch, beech, and maple from which the clothespins were manufactured. It was with that company that Clothespin Jimmy had negotiated a twenty-year timber contract calling for the delivery in his mill-yard of not less than five millions nor more than ten millions of feet of timber a year. Pursuant to this contract the new mills had been erected. Here was news indeed. What did it signify? What would be its results that touched Jim Ashe? And why had Zaanan Frame wanted him to be apprised—warned—of the event? If Zaanan's hint to read the paper was of such undoubted value, would not his other suggestion be worth looking into? Jim thought so, and inquired his way to the Widow Stickney's. She occupied a pleasant, maple-shaded house surrounded by riotous flower-beds and more practical kitchen gardens. It was attractive with the flavor of home. Jim rang the bell.

The result of his call and inspection was that he rented from the widow her second-floor front and arranged to be fed at her table. As he was leaving she hesitated, hemmed, and hawed, as Clothespin Jimmy would have put it, and finally said:

"I got one other boarder. Jest one. Hain't no objections to that, have you?"

"None whatever, Mrs. Stickney," said Jim, which was perfectly true. He had neither objections nor curiosity regarding the fact. However, as he walked between the flower-beds to the gate some one turned in and approached him. He looked up, felt himself draw a little sudden breath of surprise, for the individual was Marie Ducharme. Jim knew instantly that she was the other boarder. She passed him, cheeks slightly flushed, eyes straight ahead, without deigning to look at him. He felt a warmth about his ears.

That evening he sat late on the hotel piazza, working on a puzzle.

He could not piece it together. Why had Zaanan Frame wanted him to know of Michael Moran's new business venture? But, even more difficult of solution, why had Zaanan wanted him to board with the Widow Stickney?

Marie Ducharme insisted on obtruding herself into his puzzlings. It was absurd, he knew, but had she anything to do with the matter?

CHAPTER VI

On the day the mills commenced operating Jim Ashe called for a statement of the company's condition from Mr. Grierson. As Jim expected, it proved to be disquieting. The facts were that the mills had cost upward of two hundred thousand dollars; there was still owing for machinery and materials some thirty thousand dollars; there was seven thousand dollars cash in the bank. The weekly payroll was over two thousand dollars. Other operating expenses, with the cost of supplies and timber, brought this sum up to five thousand dollars a week—and as yet not a penny's worth of manufactured product had been turned out or shipped.

"According to this," Jim said to Mr. Grierson, "we can run a week. Then what?"

"Then," said Mr. Grierson, his voice dry and rattling like one of the leaves of his ledger, "we'll have to have some more money."

"Oh," said Jim, grimly, "that's all there is to it, eh? Well, where'll we get it? Supposing we are able to begin shipments by the end of next week—how soon can we expect returns?"

"Thirty days at the best."

"And in that thirty days we'll be spending nearly thirty thousand dollars—which we haven't got. I have heard of working capital before, but I never comprehended what a pleasant thing it was to have. Where does one get money, Grierson?"

"From the bank."

"To be sure. I guess I'm beginning to understand what father was talking about when he said he milked the business. That fifty thousand of his would make a fine plug to put in this hole. But that's gone. If I know father, he took it to make me hustle. His sense of humor works that way. Well, I'll see what I can puzzle out, Grierson."

Jim was in a measure prepared to be helmsman of his commercial ship, so far as the manufacturing and selling of his wares were concerned; but when the vessel entered financial waters, with a storm blowing and a tortuous channel to thread, he felt he ought to toot the whistle frantically and signal for a pilot. But there was no pilot to be had. There was nothing for it but to slow down and dodge through the reefs, taking frequent soundings with the lead of good judgment, striving with his eyes to pierce the vexed waters for hidden rocks. In short, the time had arrived to spread the bread of uncertainty with the butter of optimism.

He must have money. Two methods of procuring it presented themselves, but he liked the features of neither of them. The first was to borrow—if possible; the second, to sell stock. Without hesitation he eliminated the latter. He put on his hat, stopped long enough in the outer office to tell Grierson he was going to the bank, and went out.

He handed his card to Mr. Wills, cashier of the institution, and Mr. Wills shook hands with him in the manner that cashiers shake hands with individuals who are to deposit some hundreds of thousands of dollars a year with them.

"Glad to know you, Mr. Ashe. I was wondering when you'd find time to drop in to see us."

"I hope you've got lots of money, now that I am here," said Jim, with specious confidence.

"Enough to warrant us in locking the vault," said Mr. Wills. "Anything special we can do for you to-day?"

"Well," said Jim, "you could lend me a few dollars."

"Your father said you might be wanting to borrow," said Mr. Wills. "He had, as you know, of course, a conference with our board this spring, and we stand ready to do what we can for you. We're a small bank, you know. Some of our directors were against making a loan of any size to a corporation, but Zaanan Frame and Mr. Moran were in favor—which wound up that ball of string. How much will you be wanting?"

"Thirty thousand dollars," said Jim, half expecting the cashier to jump to his feet and call a strong assistant to escort him to the street.

"That's just inside the limit. Need it right away?"

"Yes."

Mr. Wills fumbled in a pigeonhole and passed Jim a note.

"Make this out, sign it as an officer of your company, and put your personal indorsement on the back. It's a demand note, you observe. We prefer that kind."

Jim wasn't clear just what the difference was between that kind and the other. It didn't matter. He was going to get the money he needed—without an effort. It was a shock to him. Were money matters arranged thus easily? Was money in considerable sums so easy to come by? He signed the note, and was told the amount would be credited to his accounts as of that day.

After he had chatted a moment, and thanked Mr. Wills as profusely as he believed it wise, he turned away. But a sudden recollection stopped him. Mr. Wills had said Zaanan Frame and Mr. Moran had favored the loan. Did you ever eat cherry pie, delicious cherry pie, and suddenly encounter a pit which the cook had overlooked? Jim felt much the same way.

"What Mr. Moran is on your board?" he asked.

Wills looked his astonishment.

"Why, Michael Moran, of course!" he said.

As Jim turned off the road on to the mill lot, a man two inches shorter than he and four inches broader accosted him.

"You're Mr. Ashe, ain't you?" the man asked.

Jim nodded and stopped. The man, who wore a calico shirt that, stout as it was, threatened to rip out at the seams when the big muscles played beneath, was an individual whose life had not fallen in places of ease. Work, hard work, had made him. He had triumphed over it. His will and a splendid body had triumphed, until Jim paid the tribute of his admiration to the result of it.

"Got any place for a cant-hook man?"

"I think we can use one in the log-yard. Out of a job?"

"Walked out of it. When I heard Mike Moran was goin' to run the Diversity Hardwood outfit I quit—sudden."

Jim waited.

"I worked for him three year back on the South Branch." The man spat savagely in the dust. "Self-respectin' lumberjack wouldn't 'a' stayed twenty-four hours gittin' what some of them fellers got. Me, it wasn't so bad. 'What was the matter?' says you. 'Plenty,' says I. First, he starts in gittin' rid of as good a crew as ever stuck their legs under a cook-shanty table, and filled up the woods with Polacks and Italians and Hunkies. Just critters with arms and laigs like folks. Grub was rotten—rotten! Them poor foreigners got it comin' and goin'. Knocked round, fed spoiled meat—and then cheated out of their pay. Oh, foreigners hain't the only ones that's been cheated out of their pay in Michigan camps. I wisht I had what was comin' to me fair, Mr. Ashe. Why, I knowed two Polacks that come out of Moran's Camp Three, after workin' from November till April—and they come out owin' him eighteen dollars!"

"Now, now," said Jim.

"I'm tellin' the truth. Wanigan. Jest robbed off'n 'em. Get a plug of tobacco at the wanigan—charged for six. Like that. And fines. No wonder he's gittin' richer 'n hell. Gittin' out his timber don't cost him nothin' to speak of. Men like him is drivin' real woodsmen out of Michigan. You can go so far with robbin' an Irishman or a Norwegian or a Nova-Scotian—and then somethin' busts. But with them lingo-talkin' foreigners, why there hain't no fight to 'em. And he'll do the same here. 'Fore another spring the camps'll be full of 'em—and him robbin' 'em. I've heard ugly things of Mike Moran. Not dealin's with men, I mean. I've had stories whispered to me by men I believed. And one I know is so. Ask somebody that knows what become of Susie Gilders. I calc'late some girl's dad or brother'll be splittin' Mike Moran with an ax one of these days. But I'm talkin' too much, Mr. Ashe. Didn't figger to git off on this rig. How about that job?"

"Report to the superintendent. Tell him I sent you. What's your name?"

"Tim Bennett."

"Well, Tim, I don't know you and you don't know me, but I'd hate to have you think about me as you do about Moran. I'll try to see you don't. These are my mills, and the crew are working for me—but that doesn't mean any man or girl is to be afraid of me. If anything goes wrong, tell me. Once I wanted to do something besides run a clothespin-mill. I wanted to see if I couldn't turn in and do something for these Polacks and Hunkies and Italians—something that would change them from being foreigners into Americans. But I couldn't have my way. But this much I can do—I can see that the folks who work for me get a square deal. You'll find the superintendent back by the log-slide."

Tim hesitated a moment, seemed to have something more to say, but to find difficulty saying it. Finally he blurted out: "Say, Mr. Ashe, I b'lieve you and me is goin' to get on."

Jim recognized the compliment; it was no small one.

"I hope so, Tim," he said.

Jim sat down in his chair before his desk and scowled at the wall. Michael Moran—everywhere that name obtruded itself—Michael Moran and Zaanan Frame. The pair of them seemed to impend over the Ashe Clothespin Company like twin thunderclouds, threatening, possessed of destructive potentialities. They had met, conferred with Morton Welliver after that gentlemen had delivered his ultimatum. Had that conference concerned him? Jim believed it had. Just what harm Zaanan Frame was potent to cause, Jim did not know; but Moran—Moran owned the little railroad, the sole outlet for Jim's wares; he controlled the lumber company from which came Jim's logs; his voice was preponderating in the bank to which Jim owed thirty thousand dollars.

A thought came to Jim: If he could buy Moran's logs and pay Moran a profit on them—and then himself manufacture them into clothespins and realize another profit—how great would be Moran's profit if in his own mills he manufactured clothespins from his own logs! Jim believed that in Moran's place he would covet the Ashe Clothespin Company. And Moran's various activities showed him to be an acquisitive individual. But nowhere had Moran manifested an unfriendly spirit; indeed, he had been distinctly friendly in the matter of the loan. What then? In any event, Jim told himself, it would not be time wasted to keep a clear eye on the man and, if possible, to rear in advance defenses against his possible attack.

Presently he got up and went into the outer office, where Grierson and his assistant were making occult entries in black and red ink on the pages of huge books. These tomes, in which were recorded the daily history of business transactions, always affected Jim with a feeling of awe, and secretly he had for Grierson and his young man a profound admiration. Anybody who could make all those entries and add all those figures, and then, a month afterward, have the slightest idea what all the agglomeration was about, was possessed of some divine spark akin to genius!

"Grierson," said Jim, "have you ever made the acquaintance of the creature known as a demand note?"

"Not personally, I thank Heaven," Grierson said, piously.

"But you know its habits?"

"You're joking, Mr. Ashe." Anything akin to humor was not to be tolerated when it touched a thing so sacred as one of the bits of business impedimenta.

"I'm exceedingly serious. What can you tell me of the habits and personal peculiarities of the thing?"

"A demand note," said Grierson, with musty gravity, "is a negotiable instrument running for an indefinite period. It differs from a time note in that it may be presented and payment demanded"—he accented the word "demanded" in a manner that Jim thought vindictive—"at any time the holder chooses. Am I clear?"

"Perfectly—and disquietingly. I am to understand that if you give a man a demand note he may drop in on you casually whenever the notion seizes him and make you—er—in the undignified language of the soap salesman, come across? Is that it?"

Mr. Grierson nodded, frowned, peered anxiously at his ledger as if he feared a figure or two might sneak away from him while his attention was distracted.

"Can you say anything cheerful about one of them?" Jim persisted.

"The only cheerful thing about a demand note, Mr. Ashe, is to know you are able to pay it whenever it turns up—which most people are not."

"That," said Jim, "is an observation made from great depths of wisdom."

"I hope, Mr. Ashe, you have not been making any demand paper."

"Your hope is vain, Grierson. The thing is done. The sword is suspended over my head. I am now speculating on the possibility of certain gentlemen cutting the hair that holds it."

He went back to his desk again with the intention of boring into the inwardness of the situation, but, strangely, his mind showed a disposition to wander. It skipped offishly away from demand notes and speculations regarding Michael Moran; was drawn again and again where Jim did not want it to go—and where it would not be welcome. Of the latter he was sure. For it was Marie Ducharme who obtruded and elbowed aside more serious matters.

Jim moved to the Widow Stickney's that night. He wondered how Miss Ducharme would regard his coming. Doubtless it would not decrease the ill will she felt toward him. Doubtless she would regard it as an impertinent intrusion. What did it matter how she regarded it? He said that to himself, but somehow he could not quite convince himself that he said it with all sincerity.

CHAPTER VII

The rural individual, riding for the first time on a descending elevator, experiences a sensation that leads to a fixed preference for stairs. It is a peculiar sensation. It may be reproduced in less degree psychologically. For instance, the boy on his way to the woodshed with his father and a razor-strop knows it; the young man about to announce to her father his ambition to become a son-in-law is acquainted with it. It comes to many people as they approach the unknown, the dreaded, the long-sought-after. It is a mingling of excitement, apprehension, anticipation, and the three of them do not mingle in peace. They seem, indeed, to have a most lively and troublesome time of it in the region known as the pit of the stomach.

As Jim left his room to go down to his first breakfast at the Widow Stickney's table he experienced an unmistakable attack of it. Marie Ducharme was the cause. Doubtless they would breakfast together. He was a bit apprehensive as to how it would go off. There was a certain amount of curiosity-incited anticipation of a second meeting with her, a second opportunity to glimpse her queer, disturbed, turbulent personality. Let there be no error here—Jim Ashe was not drawn toward Marie Ducharme. Quite the contrary. She was not at all the sort of person who would attract him; and her present frame of mind was not such as to magnetize any healthy young man. But she was a girl; she was a step beyond the ordinary; she had a personality that one could not encounter and escape unaffected. That was all.

He hesitated for a moment in the hall, and then entered the dining-room, where the widow and Marie Ducharme were already at the table.

"Right here, Mr. Ashe," said the widow; "take this here chair with the arms and the cushion into it. It'll seem sort of queer to see a man settin' into it agin. My first used it and my second used it."

"And you keep it in case it might be needed again," said Jim, gravely.

The widow shook her head. "'Tain't nothin' but a memento no more. Husbands is all right, but enough's enough. What a body can want of more 'n two is more 'n I can see. Let me make you acquainted with Miss Ducharme, Mr. Ashe."

Miss Ducharme nodded coldly.

"Cream 'n' sugar?" asked the widow.

"Some cream, a good deal of sugar, and a little coffee," said Jim, stealing a look at the young woman. She was stirring her coffee, a process which appeared to require concentration. Jim didn't blame her for stirring it or for doing anything else which would bring to public attention a hand as graceful and shapely as hers. Her face, beneath a stack of blackest hair, was expressionless.

"Mr. Ashe hain't goin' to bite you, Marie," said the widow, with a note of exasperation in her voice. Jim was glad he had not taken a swallow of coffee, for he could not have been responsible for consequences.

Miss Ducharme raised her eyes slowly, looked for an instant into Jim's eyes. "Nobody's going to bite me if I can help it," she said.

"Mrs. Stickney is right," said Jim, "I'm not vicious. I almost never bite strangers. Still, I might wear a muzzle if it would help matters."

Miss Ducharme made no reply save a faint movement of her shoulders—inherited from an ancestor who had served Frontenac. She finished her coffee and toast and egg slowly, arose silently, and left the room. The widow looked after her a moment with compressed lips.

"Sometimes," she said, "she's that cantankerous my hand fairly itches to come against her ear. Seems she might 'a' acted a leetle prettier, bein's you're a stranger and this is your first meal."

"Don't let it worry you, Mrs. Stickney."

"Worry me! Huh! 'Tain't worry that ails me, it's bein' that provoked with her. She's lived with me since her folks died. She was fifteen then. I couldn't make her out as a child and a Philadelphy lawyer couldn't make her out as a woman. She's been gittin' worse. Marie's a good girl, Mr. Ashe—better 'n a lot of these mealy-mouthed, bowin'-and-scrapin' ones—and Lord knows she's smarter. Too dum smart, I call her, for her own good. But she's queer. Kind of knurly. She don't appear to like folks, somehow."

"Possibly, Mrs. Stickney, the trouble is that she doesn't like herself."

"She gits on my mind. Sometimes I'm afeard she's goin' to mess up what chances of happiness she's got. She sets and thinks too much, and some of the things she says would fair shock you out of your shoes. If I thought she meant 'em, old as she is I'd take her acrost my knee and see if a slipper wouldn't change her point of view some."

"Anyhow, I'll promise not to quarrel with her, Mrs. Stickney," said Jim, rising. He felt it was not altogether ethical to discuss Miss Ducharme thus freely. The widow seemed to have no such scruples. Indeed, she was willing at all times and seasons to discuss anybody, absent or present, and to put into frank and expressive terms her thoughts concerning them. The widow was no gossip, no backbiter, but a woman of opinions and a nimble tongue undeterred by fear or favor.

"A husband's what she needs," said she. "One with enough disposition to go so far's to lay his hand on her if she went past his patience. I mind my first husband shakin' me once. I was young, then, with notions. Dun'no's anythin' ever done me so much good. 'Tain't considered proper no more—but if there was more shakin's there'd be fewer divorcin's."

"Perhaps our men are deteriorating under the influences of modern life," Jim suggested, with a twinkle in his eye. "The headship of the family is passing to the other sex."

"Then men ought to be up and doin' somethin' about it," said the widow. "I wouldn't give shucks for a man that let a woman run him. All this here talk about emancipatin' wimmin makes me sick to my stummick. Wimmin don't need emancipatin'. What they need is bossin'. I've been a woman consid'able of a spell and I calc'late I ought to know."

"I think my grandmother would agree with you if she were living."

"Of course. I'm grandmother to six. My idee is that wimmin don't git settled and sensible till they turn sixty."

"I'm in favor of giving the vote to all grandmothers."

"It would fetch consid'able sense into elections," said the widow. "Don't hurry off. I like to talk—maybe you've noticed it."

"And enjoyed it," said Jim, passing through the door.

Miss Ducharme was putting on her hat in the hall. Jim's first thought was to pass on without pause; his second and better thought was to parley.

"I'm waving a flag of truce, Miss Ducharme," he said. "Can't we declare an armistice for ten minutes to bury our dead?"

"I have no war with you," she replied, with no interest. "I simply don't like you. Why should we talk about it?"

"There'll be no trouble on that score," said Jim, smiling. He rather enjoyed her acerbity. "You see, I'm not exactly fond of you. But we're living under the same roof and eating at the same table. If we could agree on a truce or a pretense that we are not distasteful to each other—merely while we're in the house—it might make Mrs. Stickney's life a bit more joyous. I assure you that if I had known you lived here I shouldn't have intruded."

"Mrs. Stickney has a right to take whatever boarders she chooses."

"I'm not asking you to be friends—" Jim stopped. He was conscious of that feeling of sudden determination, of that urge to quick action which had come upon him several times since his arrival in Diversity, of that spirit which had earned for him among his workmen the name of Sudden Jim. So he cut off his sentence and started another.

"I'm going to be your friend, whether you like it or not. Possibly I shall even like you. You seem to need friends, if what you said to me the other day is an indication of what is really going on inside you. The matter is out of your hands. You said absurd things; things dangerous for any young woman to say, even if she knows in her heart they're ridiculous."

"They were not absurd. I meant them. You had no business to be there to hear—to know. You let me talk when I was unstrung. You spied—it amounted to that."

"Let it stand that way. I do know and I'm going to meddle. You hate Diversity because it isn't New York City. You talk recklessly to a stranger. The sum of the matter is that you are steering for a big unpleasantness. If you don't like things as they are, what is the sense of putting in your time making them worse? Pretty soon you'll talk and think and gloom yourself into doing something that'll smash the china. So I'm going to meddle. Of course I don't know you, and I haven't any personal interest in you. But I'm interested in you as a sociological specimen. As such I'm going to be polite to you, and as entertaining as possible while we're at Mrs. Stickney's table. I shall expect you to be humanly polite to me. Do you understand?"

She looked at him queerly, almost apprehensively. When she replied her voice was low, not cold, not friendly. Jim's will had encountered her will and been the stronger.

"Yes," she said.

"You'll be reasonably decent—so Mrs. Stickney won't lose her appetite?"

"Yes. In the house. But nowhere else. And I shall hate you—hate you."

"That's enough for a beginning."

"And don't you dare to watch me. Don't dare to pry into my affairs. Don't dare to interfere with me in any way."

"Miss Ducharme, if you fell into the river it would be only human for me to fish you out. Drowning isn't the worst thing there is. Folks who would jump into the water after you would stand by and let trouble come to you which would make you wish you could drown. A man has the right to interfere. Humanity gives it to him. It's silly to think I have the right to save your life from a physical danger, but haven't the right to save you from the other kind. You say it's none of my business. It is my business. What threatens any human being is the business of every other human being, if he weren't too lazy or too hidebound or too conventional to admit it. You have brains—or you wouldn't be in the state of mind you are. You know logic when you meet it face to face—and that was logic. The trouble with you is ambition that has fermented in the can."

"You are a bumptious young man," she said, hotly. "You're full of school-book theories. What do you know about a woman? About her problems? What do you know about anything? You haven't lived yet. I'm a dozen years older than you—in knowing what the world is. You talked idealistic nonsense the other day about the good there is in the world; you're talking idealistic nonsense to-day. You're a cub altruist. What you think is humanitarianism is merely impertinence. Altruism is just a word in the dictionary."

"I knew you had brains," said Jim, "and I'll bet you disagree with Mrs. Stickney about woman's sphere. She says every woman ought to be bossed by a man—and shouldn't be allowed the vote till she's a grandmother."

"I don't agree. A woman is an individual, complete—she needs no man for a complement. Her abilities are as great, her potentialities as strong, She has the right to own herself, to guard herself, to reach out for the life she wants as a man does. Because her risk in life is greater she has the right to more than equality; she has the right to special privilege and special protection. She has the right to demand that she be put in a condition where she can protect her treasures, material, physical, spiritual. And how can she do it as things are? Less than half the world—in trousers—holds the majority in captivity, exercising the rights of conquerors. You make laws to bind us. Men make laws respecting the peculiar problems of women—when men know less of women and their problems than they do of the mound-builders. We don't ask to make your laws—only men can make laws for men; but we do demand to make our own laws. We demand that weapons be placed in our hands for our own defense. With some of the theories I do not agree, but I do insist that women should not be left—in the condition they are now—as the women of a sacked city, at the mercy of the conquerors."

"You have thought, haven't you? Perhaps not altogether healthily, but keenly. Dinner-table conversations won't be trite."

"Thought! What has there been to do in Diversity but think? And the more I think, the more I comprehend, the worse the handcuffs cut into my wrists. Some day it will become unendurable."

"And then," Jim said, "I shall jump into the water after you. We'll take altruism out of the dictionary for that one time, anyhow."

She said nothing, moved toward the door.

"Our agreement is sealed?" he asked. "We are to act toward each other like ordinarily polite human beings while we are in the house?"

"Yes," she said over her shoulder.

"Are we to shake hands on it?"

"No," she said, sharply, and went out, carrying herself lightly, with splendid poise, eye-delighting grace.

Jim felt a tinge of regret that her face was not lovely. With the intellect that was hers, he thought gravely, with her beauty of line and motion, beauty of face would have made her a miracle. But she was no miracle. She was a small, over-burdened, vainly protesting girl who had fought her way alone to such ideals as she possessed. With her will she thought she had molded her own soul. She did not know that souls are never subject to finite processes; she did not know that each soul is a single drop from the great ocean of Divinity, coming to us in such purity as the great ocean possesses, to be made more pure or to be defiled by our acts—but never to be altered by our wills. One day would come when she would call up her soul before her and know it as she did not know it now.

Jim's final thought on the matter was that Marie was not a modern woman, not an advanced woman, but a primitive woman, an atavism, fighting as her remotest mother must have fought for the very right to be.

CHAPTER VIII

The mills started as well as any new mills could be expected to start. They did not run perfectly; minor defects developed, machines ran stiffly, hot-boxes developed, belts required tightening; but Jim Ashe was willing to praise his millwrights for good work done. As he walked through the big plant between rows of machines which chugged or punched or sawed rhythmically; as he watched hardwood logs crawl up the slide at the rear of the mill, and pass through a multitude of processes to emerge into the warehouse finished clothespins or dishes or bowls, he felt a sense of pride in the thing he was doing. He was drawing straight from Nature to minister to the necessities of man. It was no ignoble task.

If profits came to him, they would be honestly earned profits, the results of labor. He was not wasting as timber had been wasted before his day. Every scrap of wood that came into his mill was utilized. Modern machinery made possible a saving in timber that thirty years ago would have run into hundreds of millions of feet of pine, had the pioneer wasters availed themselves of it. Thin band-saws turned a minimum of each log into ashes; with them Jim got seven boards where old-time circular saws had been able to give but six. Resaws redeemed the slabs, took from them the finest gold of the timber which lay just under the bark. In other days slab-piles had been known to burn constantly for years, a savage waste. Sawdust, remnants of slabs, edgings furnished the fuel which gave him his power. Here was nothing of which to be ashamed; much to justify pride. Here was an enterprise a man might defend before the court of posterity.

But if the mills ran to Jim's satisfaction at first they did not improve as he demanded. In ten days from the beginning there swept over the plant a pestilence of mishaps, each mishap causing the shutdown of a department, sometimes of the whole mill. It did not abate, but continued maddeningly. The shrill toot of the little whistle which commanded the engineer to stop motion became a throb in a sore tooth to Jim. Each accident was small; the total of them reached dangerous magnitude.

Jim called in Nelson, head millwright, and his superintendent, John Beam. They came wearing the faces of harried men.

"In three days," Jim said, shortly, "we've lost five hours in shut-downs. Why?"

"Every night," said Nelson, "we inspect every belt, every pulley, every gear, every machine. We make sure nothing is wrong—and next day a dozen things go wrong.

"The last shut-down was for a split pulley on the main shaft. I went over that shaft last night myself. That pulley was as tight and sound as any pulley could be. And it twisted off this morning. We had to shut down yesterday to fix the main driving-belt. Four rivets had come loose and she'd have pulled clean apart. There wasn't a sign of a loose rivet night before last—I'd take my oath on it." He looked gloomily out of the window. The thing was twanging on his nerves as well as on Jim's.

"John and I aren't trying to make excuses for ourselves. We'd be tickled to death to take the blame if we could only fix it on to ourselves. What makes me want to roll over and howl is that we can't fix it any place. In spite of all we can do these things happen. It's just as he says about what he's seen. Things I know were sound and in perfect runnin' condition at night goes wrong in the mornin'. And how in blazes are we goin' to explain the nails?"

"What nails?" Jim asked.

"In the logs. Every sawyer expects to find some nails when he's sawin' maple. Especially in a sugar country. They was drove in to hold sap buckets. But a man don't expect to find 'em in beech and birch—and he don't expect to find brand-new ten-penny nails, neither. The saw-filer's tearin' his hair. If it keeps on we won't have a saw to cut with in the big mill. You know what a nail'll do to a saw, Mr. Ashe."

"Why doesn't the sawyer keep his eyes open for them?" Jim snapped.

"Keep his eyes open! Mr. Ashe, before he puts a log on the carriage now he goes over it from end to end. You can't see a nail that's countersunk so the head's half an inch in."

"The way you say that sounds as if you meant something. Out with it."

"I mean," said Nelson, doggedly, "that it looks to me as if somebody was plantin' them nails so's we'd saw into 'em. I mean it looks to me like somebody sneaked in here and tampered with things after we get through inspectin'. I mean that the things that's happened in this mill couldn't 'a' happened without bein' helped to happen." John Beam nodded his head in agreement.

"That's nonsense," Jim said, emphatically.

"Maybe it is. Maybe a crazy man's doin' it. But, Mr. Ashe, it's bein' done. I know it as well as if I'd seen the feller doin' it."

"How about the watchmen?"

"All of 'em worked for us in the old mills. 'Tain't none of them. I'd take my Bible oath on that."

Jim sat silent a moment, scowling at the floor.

"You men know what shut-downs mean," he said. "Here's five hours in three days—half a day's time gone. That means a loss in wages alone of a hundred dollars, which is a small part of it. It's got to stop. I don't care whether these accidents are accidents or whether somebody is arranging them-they've got to quit, and quit sudden. Suppose we lose a hundred dollars every three days. That's two hundred a week and ten thousand a year. Have you talked about this to anybody?"

"No," said Nelson.

Beam shook his head,

"Is there any talk in the mill?"

"Haven't heard any."

"Well, keep quiet about it. If you fellows are right, we don't want to advertise it. Now clear out of here and do the best you can. Keep your eyes open. Don't get suspicious of anybody till you have mighty good reason. I'd hate to think it was any of the crew."

"It's somebody that knows the run of things."

"Yes."

"What possible reason could anybody have, Mr. Ashe—"

"That'll be my job—to find out. This suspicion of yours is upsetting. I want to think about it. Then I'll do something."

Nelson's eyes twinkled as he glanced sideways at Beam. As they went out Jim heard him say in a low tone:

"You bet he'll do somethin'—and it'll come sudden and astonishin'. Sudden Jim!" There was a note of affection in Nelson's voice as he pronounced the name.

Jim settled down to think about it. That some one was planning deliberately to cripple the plant by injuring its machinery was illogical. It affronted Jim's reason. Yet it was a theory impossible to dismiss. It must be considered. In that case, who had an adequate motive? Nobody, so far as Jim could see at first glance.

He set up the possibilities, only to knock them down one by one. It might be the work of a man with a mania for malicious destruction. Highly improbable, thought Jim. It might be workmen or a workman with a grievance practising sabotage. But so far as Jim knew there was no discontent; the crew were satisfied; there had been no complaints, no unrest. That possibility must be dismissed. It might be some individual in Diversity with a grudge to work off against the company. But Jim had never heard of conflict between the company and a citizen, nor had unfriendliness developed since his arrival. This, too, was dismissed.

Who had an interest in the failure of the concern? A thought which lay deep in his mind, which he had hoped to conceal even from himself, obtruded: the Clothespin Club. As an organization of men who had fought upward through adverse conditions, against obstacles, side by side with his father, Jim did not believe them guilty. But organizations of honorable business men often employ underlings, concerning whose methods their masters neglect to make close inquiry. Might this not be the case? It was the sole possibility to stand erect before Jim's reason.

The Club brought up speculations on Morton J. Welliver—which led to Michael Moran and Zaanan Frame. They led to the Diversity Hardwood Company, of which Moran was now the head. Should the Ashe Clothespin Company fail, who was most likely to succeed it? Who would be in the best position to take over the wreck and operate it? To that question there was but one answer—the Diversity Hardwood Company. Now Jim became obsessed by a real suspicion—and he would act upon it until evidence showed him he was at fault. He would move on the theory that Welliver, Moran, and Frame were not clean of hand. Frame! What had he to base a suspicion of Zaanan Frame upon? Nothing but an evident acquaintance with Welliver, a patent closeness of relations to Moran. No, the old justice's name must stand among the suspected.

"Where's Mr. Ashe?" roared an angry voice in the outer office.

Jim heard Grierson's parchment voice give the direction, and heavy feet pounded down the hall to his door. Watson, foreman of the veneer room, burst in, a huge veneer knife in his arms—no mean weight. "Look at that," he said, belligerently, dropping the knife on Jim's desk with a bang. "Look at that! Two knives this mornin'."

There was plain to view a generous nick on the cutting edge.

"What did it?" Jim asked.

"Nail. Twice this mornin'. Now I've got to shut down one lathe till the other knife's ground down. What land of timber is this, anyhow, with nails hid all over it?"

"Nothing the matter with your eyesight, is there?"

Watson glared at Jim, shook a grimy finger at him.

"I kin see nails as far as anybody, but I can't look through an inch of timber to 'em. We always look out for nails, but it's easy to see 'em. Bolts come to us from the vats with the bark peeled, and mostly the peelers get the nails with their spuds. But nobody kin see a nail that's sunk an inch and the hole plugged. Yes, sir, that's what I mean. The hole was plugged!"

"How do you know?"

"Strip of veneer showed it. Slice of plug was still stickin' in. And we went over a dozen more bolts with a fine-tooth comb. We found one with a spot in it that looked suspicious. Dug it out and it was a plug! And we notched in and hit the nail. Now what does that mean?"

"It means you're to keep your mouth shut about it, and tell some kind of a story to your gang to keep their mouths shut."

"Somebody's goin' to get hurt," Watson said, darkly.

"Yes," said Jim, slowly, "somebody is going to get hurt—bad."

"I s'pose I'll have to look over every bolt with opery-glasses," growled Watson.

"I'll give you a man who is to do nothing else. Tell Beam I said so."

Jim put on his coat and hat and went to dinner. His physical machine was such that it required nourishment, no matter what was happening to the mental department. Some men lose their appetites when things go wrong. Not so Jim Ashe. Some men drown their troubles in drink. Jim had his drowned three times daily in hunger.

When he had eaten his dinner—for the Widow Stickney had only vaguely heard of a strange custom of moving that meal along till six o'clock and having a thing at noon called luncheon; to her, luncheon was something you put up in a basket and took to a picnic—he leaned back in his chair for his usual midday chat with the old lady.

"You've lived here long, Mrs. Stickney?"

"Born in the county."

"You ought to be pretty well acquainted with folks hereabout."

"Don't have to live here long to be that. Everybody you meet is boilin' over with anxiety to give you the true life history of everybody else. You kin git to know Diversity consid'able well in a week, if you're willin' to listen."

"Justice Frame's lived here a long time, too, hasn't he?"

"Him and me was children together."

"Mrs. Stickney, I'm not asking this wholly out of curiosity. I'm new to you all. I've got my hands pretty full, and there are people in the world who would be glad to see me spill part of my load. It's a fine thing to know whom you can depend on and whom you want to shy at. So I'm asking you to tell me something about Zaanan Frame."

"He's a stiff-spined old grampus," said the widow, promptly. "Him and me squabbles so's the neighbors 'most come a-runnin' in to part us. He's powerful set on havin' his own way—and mostly he gits it. He's sharper 'n a new sickle. He's been justice of the peace here since before Mary Whittaker was born, and Mary's got a boy of ten herself. Hain't never been nothin' more 'n just justice of the peace, but he runs the whole blessed county out of his office. He's one of them things the papers call a political boss; but if I do say it, Zaanan Frame does a good job of it. But he runs it so folks git the wuth of their taxes, and so that them that wants justice gits it.

"About dependin' on him," she went on, after drawing a breath, "you won't never find him dodgin' about underhand. If he likes you, he hain't apt to show it by runnin' up and kissin' you in public; and if he don't like you, he don't cuss you and try to hit you with a pebble whenever you meet—but you soon git to know. I've knowed him to give a man he didn't like all the best of a deal—so nobody'd accuse him of workin' a personal spite. I've knowed him to refuse things to a friend he'd 'a' done for a stranger. They say he stretches the powers of his office and does things a justice hain't got no right to do—and I calc'late he does. But it's in time of need for somebody. He meddles into folkses' fam'ly affairs, and plans to marry off this girl to that feller—which plans mostly works out to his notion.

"He's got a sort of notion he was put here by God Almighty to be father and mother to every man, woman, and child in the county. But there hain't no complaints of him as a parent, though he's a mean-dispositioned, meddlin', sharp-tongued, stubborn-minded old coot.

"Diversity hain't given much to sayin' anythin' but meannesses about folks; we don't speak none about Zaanan, but I calc'late there's growed men that'll walk behind him to the cemetery with tears a-runnin' down their cheeks, and wimmin that'll be sobbin' and leetle children that'll know what it means to lose their pa. If there's any argument when Zaanan gits to stand before the great white throne, he's got a right to say: 'Wait a minnit, Lord, till we kin git in a number of souls that's here but was bound for the other place till I got my hands on the reins.' If you're worryin' as to where Zaanan Frame stands, I kin tell you—he stands where it's honestest and lightest for him to stand. My goodness! but hain't I been goin' on about him! Thinkin' as high of him as I do, it's a wonder I don't up and make him my third."

Jim sat gnawing his finger silently for many minutes after the widow was done speaking. She spoke as one who knew. Jim knew she would have testified in a court of law just as she had spoken to him. Nor would she have spoken so except from certainty. He was compelled, therefore, to revise his judgments and suspicions.

"If you were in a hard place, Mrs. Stickney, and needed advice, would you go to Zaanan Frame?"

"I'd hitch up and go at a gallop," she said.

"That," said Jim, "is about what I think I'll do."

CHAPTER IX

Jim rapped on the door of Zaanan Frame's office. At the last minute he had been of two minds whether he should go in or pass on about his business. The sound of his own knuckles on the panel decided him.

"Come in," called Zaanan's voice.

Jim entered and saw the old justice sitting behind his desk, a sheep-bound volume propped up before him. Over the top of this a pair of sharp blue eyes shaded by bushy eyebrows, each of which would have gladdened the heart of an ambitious young roan could he have had it for a mustache, peered at Jim.

"Huh!" snorted Zaanan.

"You've made it pretty evident," Jim said, stiffly, "that you don't like me. I can't say I have felt any uncontrollable affection for you—"

"Whoa there!" said Zaanan, closing his book, Tiffany's *Justices' Guide*, which he maintained to be the greatest contribution to human knowledge, especially of the law, since Moses received the tablets of stone. "Young feller, if you hain't too young to learn, lemme tell you it's possible to ketch more flies with maple sugar than you kin with stummick bitters. Jest smooth down the hair along your back and don't go walkin' round me stiff-legged like a dog lookin' for a fight." Zaanan's eyes twinkled. "Now, then, set and onbosom yourself."

"I've come to see you, Judge, because I have been assured that friend or enemy can trust you—"

"The Widder Stickney's been flappin' her wings and cacklin'," observed Zaanan. "Um! I figgered you'd be to see me—or else you wouldn't. Gittin' ready to kick out, but you need a wall to lean against, eh?"

"Kick out? What makes you think I'm getting ready to kick out? And at whom?"

"'Whom,'" quoted Zaanan. "I've heard of that there word. It's grammar, hain't it, but I dun'no's I ever expected to hear it spoke in Diversity. How's the meals to the widder's?"

"Very good, indeed," said Jim, nonplussed.

"You hain't the only boarder, I hear tell."

"No; Miss Ducharme is there, too."

"I want to know," said Zaanan, his eyes twinkling again. "Makes it pleasanter, I calc'late—you two young folks together."

"I think Miss Ducharme could bear up under the blow if I were to board some place else."

"Um!" said Zaanan. "Mill hain't runnin' very good, I hear."

"That's what I came to see you about—that and other things."

"Good mill, hain't it? New machines? Ought to run, hadn't it?"

"It ought to and it's going to. But, Judge, it looks a lot as if somebody didn't want it to."

"Um! That might mean consid'able and it might mean nothin'. Accordin' to my notion one of the easiest ways of givin' information is to think up words that mean what you want to tell and then to say 'em. Beatin' round the bush may scare up a rabbit, but you hain't huntin' rabbits. Eh?"

"Well, then, somebody has been tampering with our machinery to make it break down. Somebody has been driving nails into our logs to dull our saws. Whoever it is has made us shut down five hours in the last three days."

"You figger somebody's doin' it deliberate?"

"Yes."

"Got any proof?"

Jim laid before the old man such evidence as he had, but it was sufficient. Zaanan wagged his head.

"Calc'late there hain't no doubt of it. Suspect anybody special?"

"I haven't any suspicion who is working the mischief, but I have an idea he isn't doing it for himself."

"Somebody's hirin' him to do it, you mean?"

"Yes."

"Who might it be?"

"There are only two interests who would have any motive in breaking me. One is the organization of clothespin manufacturers. I'm in a fight with them now because they wanted to run my business. The other is the Diversity Hardwood Company."

"Hum! I figgered from what Welliver said a spell back that he wasn't tickled to death with you and your doin's. You hain't a bit afraid who you're suspicious of, be you?"

"I've got to be suspicious of everybody—and I'm going to be till I know who can be trusted."

"Kind of suspected me a mite, eh? Figgered I was tarred with the Welliver and Moran stick?"

"I got to thinking pretty hard when I saw you with them the morning after my row with Welliver. You seemed to be pretty good friends."

"Calc'late we be. Knowed 'em a long time."

"Judge, you don't need any more to show you I've a bad situation to deal with. I came to you—I don't just know why I came to you. On impulse, I expect."

"Sudden Jim," said Zaanan, with a chuckle.

"You've heard that, eh?"

"Yes. You was sayin' you come to me on impulse. Must 'a' figgered I'd be some use to you. Nobody'd climb a greased pole if 'twa'n't for the five-dollar bill tacked on top of it. Was you wantin' advice or money or the loan of my shot-gun?"

"I think," said Jim, slowly, "that what brought me here was a vague sort of hope of finding a friend. When a fellow's up against a fight he feels lonesome. He likes to know there's somebody besides himself to depend on. I had no reason to expect it—quite the contrary, perhaps. Anyhow, I believe you could help me with this particular problem if you wanted to."

"Young feller, a justice of the peace has a heap of duties, some set down in the statutes and some that just come nat'ral. I've been justice more 'n thirty year, and I calc'late them duties that no legislature ever thought up is the most important. F'r instance, I married Kitty Fox and Pliny Hearter. That was consid'able of a transaction; but it was consid'able more of one to git 'em back to lovin' and trustin' after they'd started runnin' round for a lawyer to git 'em a divorce. The law don't give me the right to do quite a stretch of the meddlin' I do; but it sort of appertains to this here office, and I do it. You don't want nothin' of me that's printed in law-books. So far's bein' your friend—why, I hain't makin' no sich agreements. Friends hain't made by writin' out contracts to that effect. I hain't seen enough of you to git to yearnin' over you. But I'll ease your mind some on one p'int—I hain't actively concerned to do you no harm. Also, I hain't got no prejudices ag'in you."

Jim shrugged his shoulders. "It was a ridiculous sort of notion for me to come like this, without any idea what I wanted. I need help, but what kind of help I don't know. Anyhow, I'm glad you're not with the enemy, whoever they are."

"You mentioned names—on suspicion. One of the onhealthiest habits a man ever got into. I've knowed folks to die of it. You've figgered out for yourself who's after your pelt, and why. But you hain't got no more proof than ol' man Simpkins had when he wanted me to git leetle Georgie Reed up before me for stealin' melons. The ol' man missed a big melon—next day Georgie was bein' doctored for stummick-ache. 'Twa'n't out of reason. It was evidence I was willin' to weigh and pass on in private. I calc'late Georgie et that melon. But as a court of law I couldn't do nothin' but declare Simpkins 'u'd have to show plainer proofs. That's your fix. But, young feller, if I was you I calc'late I'd kinder keep my specs wiped clean and I wouldn't let my hair grow down over my ears to speak of. G'-by."

Jim was astonished. Never had he been thus bruskly dismissed. He strode out of the office; but a sense of humor came to his rescue. He turned and bade the old justice good afternoon. Zaanan did not appear to hear.

Zaanan turned the pages of Tiffany's *Justices' Guide* for fifteen minutes after Jim's departure. Then he raised his voice in a call for Dolf Springer. Dolf, it happened, was whittling on Zaanan's doorstep. It was his custom to do so during Zaanan's office hours, for Dolf desired greatly to be useful to the dictator of Diversity County's politics. Dolf's ambition carried him so high as to make him covet the office of pathmaster. Therefore he lay in wait for opportunities to serve Zaanan.

"Perty busy, Dolf?" Zaanan asked. "Time all took up to-day?"

"Got a while to spare, Judge."

"Think of takin' a drive, Dolf? Eh? Was that what you was plannin' on?"

"I was goin' out for a spell."

"Um! What direction, Dolf? Didn't happen to be goin' out the River Road, did you?"

"That's exactly where I was goin'. Had a errant out that way."

"Take you far, Dolf? So far you couldn't git back to-night?"

"It might, Judge."

"Wa'n't goin' far's Gilder's, was you—up back of the Company's Camp Three?"

"Goin' a leetle past there, Judge."

"Um! Know Gilders?"

"Calc'late to."

"If you was to see him, Dolf, d' you figger on stoppin' for a chat? And if you do, what be you goin' to talk about?"

"I'd mention I hadn't seen him for a long spell."

"To be sure."

"And I'd mention I seen you to-day."

"Uh-huh. S'pose it would occur to you to say somethin' to the effect that it looked like business was pickin' up and stirrin' times was comin'? Eh? And that fellers with an ax to grind had better git out the grindstone? Eh?"

"Come to think of it, I guess I'd make some sich observation."

"And would you kind of speak about the new clothespin-mill? And allude to how the whistle's always tootin' for it to shut down on account of somethin' bustin'?"

"It 'u'd be int'restin' news to Gilders."

"'Twouldn't be any more 'n nat'ral for you to wonder what was the cause of it? Eh? Might suggest that somebody up his way could explain it. 'Twouldn't be s'rprisin', would it?"

"Likely to be so," said Dolf.

"G'-by, Dolf," said Zaanan.

"G'-by, Judge," said Dolf.

In ten minutes Dolf was driving a livery rig out the River Road. A twelve-mile ride lay before him, and he did not lag. Some hours later he stopped, tied his horse to a tree by the roadside and plunged into the woods—jack-pine, scrub-oak, underbrush. Fifteen minutes' scrambling brought him to an insignificant clearing with a log shanty in the middle of it. He stopped cautiously and looked about. Then he called: "Steve! Hey, Steve Gilders!"

A man, perhaps forty-five years old, stood by the shanty door. A moment before the space had been empty. He did not seem to come to that spot from anywhere, but simply to be there all at once. He was what our grandmothers would have called a "fine figger" of a man. Upward of six feet two inches he was, and handsome of feature. The handsomeness was marred by a somberness, a sternness of demeanor.

The admiration he excited was chilled by the rifle he carried under his arm—and the manner in which he carried it. It explained why Dolf had taken the precaution to call before he ventured near.

"What's wanted?" inquired Gilders.

"Zaanan Frame sent me."

The man's face relaxed. "Then you're welcome. Come in."

Dolf followed him. "Zaanan sent a message, but I can't make head or tail to it," he said.

"Probably 'twa'n't intended you should," said Gilders.

"Anyhow," Dolf said, "Zaanan he told me to come a-drivin' out here and say to you that fellers with a ax to grind had better git their grindstone out; and that business was pickin' up and stirrin' times was ahead; and that the new clothespin-mill was havin' trouble with its machinery and somebody up this here way might be able to explain what was the matter. Don't seem like much of a message to drive twelve miles to deliver."

"Huh! Goin' right back?"

"Zaanan acted like he wanted me to stay till mornin'."

"Git your hoss then. You kin sleep here."

Dolf went obediently after his animal. Steve Gilders shut his eyes and smiled. It was a peculiar thing to see. Somehow it was not reassuring, but exceedingly sinister. He had read Zaanan's message correctly. He knew what to do.

When Dolf came back Gilders was gone, nor did Dolf see his host again that night. But that worried Dolf very little. Indeed, it must be said he slept more comfortably for Gilders's absence.

At sunrise Gilders appeared out of the woods, strode lithely into the shanty, laboriously wrote a letter to Zaanan—which he sealed carefully—and delivered it to Dolf.

"I calc'late you'd better make tracks for town," he said.

Dolf did not argue the matter.

CHAPTER X

When Jim Ashe returned to the mill after his conversation with Zaanan Frame he found the machinery idle, employees pouring out of the entrances. He walked past them and into the building in a frame of mind that would have rendered him undesirable as a dinner companion. Another breakdown!

He found Nelson and Beam standing below a couple of mechanics who were working over a pair of big gears. They only nodded curtly at his approach, for apparently their patience, like Jim's, was close to the fusing-point.

"Now what?" Jim asked.

"Core gear. Stripped the wooden teeth out of it."

"How?"

Nelson shrugged his shoulders, but Beam replied. "Just got started after dinner," he said. "I was standin' not ten feet from here when I seen that solid gear lift up into the air, it looked like two foot, and come down smash onto the wooden teeth. Twouldn't be so bad if we had a spare set of teeth, but we hain't."

"Got to cut 'em out," supplemented Nelson.

"How long does that mean?"

"If we work all night we ought to get to runnin' by noon to-morrow—with luck."

"Who's to blame?" Jim demanded

"Who drove the nails in the logs?" John Beam replied, a trifle sullenly. "Nelson went over those gears last night. I seen him. He says there wa'n't anythin' wrong then."

Jim set his teeth; the urge to action came over him that had earned him the name of Sudden Jim. He recognized it, expected himself to do something decisive—and was surprised that he did not. Instead he found himself reflecting coolly, choosing the better from the worse course of action.

"It can't be helped now, boys," he said. "Speed up and get her going again—and keep quiet about it."

He turned on his heel and went up to the office, where he found the noon mail on his desk. The first letter he opened was the resignation of his salesman for New York and New England, a man of exceptional ability, whose sales mounted to many car-loads a year, and whose customers were his customers, not those of the Ashe Clothespin Company. Winkleman could take them with him to whatever firm he had sold his services. Jim knew well Winkleman had not abandoned the woodenware trade—he had gone over to Welliver or some other of the enemy. Here, Jim recognized, was the shrewdest blow of the war.

Jim went on opening his mail. Another letter was from Silvers, his Chicago representative. This man handled the product of Jim's mills as a part of his brokerage business. He was able; no week passed that did not see at least one car-load consigned to him or to his customers.

> What's up? (the letter said). Welliver wants me to drop you and come over to him. Says your goose is cooked and offers me an extra two and a half per cent. commission. Says you started this clothespin rumpus. Had a contract ready for me to sign, and wanted me to drop you unsight and unseen, I wouldn't do it, but his offer is tempting.

There was more to the communication, but here we have the heart of it. One blow followed another. The attack had commenced in earnest and Jim was on the defensive. He had declared war, but had not struck a blow. Now he must act swiftly, intelligently, efficiently. First he wired Silvers:

> Won't meet Welliver's offer. We're sound. If you can't stick by us in fight don't want you anyhow. Want men can depend on. Wire answer.

Next he called in Grierson.

"What percentage of our business is in New York and New England?" he asked.

"A quarter, maybe."

"Who sells heaviest there?"

"Plum and Mannikin."

"One of them has hired away Winkleman."

Grierson made a crisp, crackling sound with his lips. It indicated dismay. Jim smiled grimly.

"We're going to increase our Eastern business," he said. "We haven't pushed it as we might, just as those Eastern factories haven't pushed for orders in the West. But we're going to. We're going after all we can get anywhere we can get it. It's three o'clock. I want you to catch the six-o'clock train for Buffalo. Then New York and Boston. Go and pack. By the time you're back here I'll have your instructions ready for you."

"But, Mr. Ashe—"

"Hustle," said Jim. It was Sudden Jim speaking now.

In an hour Grierson was back, dubious, flustered.

"Grierson," said Jim, "you know the personnel of the woodenware business better than I. Here's what I want you to do: Land the best woodenware broker in Buffalo to handle our line for the city and western New York. Get him! Give him seven and a half commission, if necessary. Have him sign a contract like Levine's in Cleveland. Then hit for New York. There'll be soreness somewhere over this Winkleman business. It must have cut into somebody's territory. You know who to go to. We want the biggest—somebody with a sales organization. Offer them all New York and all New England outside of Boston. If they hang out for Boston, give it to them, too. If they don't insist on it go to Boston and repeat the dose. I want somebody who will sell our goods—and keep us hustling to fill orders. We'll put a dent in Plum and Mannikin. Now you'll want to bury your young man in directions for his guidance while you're gone. Get at it. And don't come back here unless you've got what I want."

Grierson was blinking. "Your father was a swift mover when he was r'iled," said he; "but for suddenness, and for landing a hard punch, I guess you are a little ahead of him. I'll do my best, Mr. Ashe."

Jim's next move was a wire to Philadelphia. Pennsylvania was the home ground of the Jenkins mills, and Jim was determined to hit as many heads as he could. Any woodenware man worthy of the name was familiar with the house of Sands & Stein, of the Quaker City. Jim's wire said:

> If interested handing our whole line Pennsylvania exclusive territory wire.

These things accomplished, Jim entered upon the routine of his work, which occupied him until six o'clock was near. Just as he was leaving the office a telegram arrived from Silvers.

"I'm no quitter," it said, tersely, and Jim knew that he had found at least one dependable man.

As Jim approached he saw a man seated on the Widow Stickney's porch. He wondered if the widow was entering on a campaign to conquer her "third," and had invited him to supper as an opening gun. Jim was not familiar enough with Diversity's citizens yet to identify an individual by his legs, and this one's face was concealed by the climbing vine. If Jim had been a native of the village he would have experienced no such difficulty, for Diversity's male inhabitants were as easy to distinguish by their pants as by their faces. We recognize a man by his face because that is the face he has always worn. The same rule held true of Diversity's trousers. Old Clem Beagle still went to church in the garments that covered him when he was married sixty years before.

When Jim climbed the porch he was convinced that the widow had nothing whatever to do with the visitor. It was Michael Moran, and Jim wondered just who in that house was responsible for his presence.

"How do you do, Mr. Ashe?" said Moran, rising and extending his hand. "I just learned you were boarding here. Glad to hear it. Makes it more interesting for Miss Ducharme, I imagine, and she needs cheering up considerable."

Jim responded to the greeting, experiencing at the same time a dubiety as to Moran's sincerity. Indeed, without any adequate reason for his belief he was of the opinion that Moran was not pleased with his presence.

"Sort of protegee of mine—Miss Ducharme. Father was walking boss for me. I always take supper with her when I'm in town, if I can manage it," Moran explained.

Jim nodded. He was remembering that it was on the morning following a visit of Michael Moran's to Diversity he had first encountered Marie, on the top of a knoll from which a view might be had of far countries. Her reckless mood, reckless words, were fresh in his mind, and he would have been glad to know if Moran had anything to do with the matter.

"Everything starting off well at the mill?"

"Very well, indeed," said Jim.

"I see you've started shipments. Hope you've been getting cars as you wanted them. If you ever have any difficulty, just let me know."

"Thank you," said Jim. His mind was only casually on what Moran was saying; it was striving to penetrate to what he was thinking. From the morning of his first sight of the man Jim had been repelled by him. That, of course, was to be laid to the fact that Moran was first seen in company with Welliver. But since then Jim had been led to suspect him as an active enemy. Stories—gossip, perhaps—that came to his ears led him to set Moran down as a shifty individual, a man who looked to the right and unexpectedly threw his brick to the left. Also he had heard from Tim

Bennett and others hints regarding Moran's attitude toward women. But there was proof of nothing. Jim was fair enough to admit this. All was hint, rumor, or deduction from flimsy bases.

"You know, of course, that I've taken over the control of the Diversity Hardwood Company?"

"I had heard it."

"That and my railroad will bring us in touch considerable. Before long we ought to hit on some sort of basis so we can work together for the benefit of both of us. We're in a position to help each other in a dozen ways."

"By driving nails in each other's logs," Jim thought, but he smiled and agreed that co-operation seemed advisable.

"Conditions in the county aren't what they ought to be," said Moran after puffing briefly on his cigar. "You and I—with the influence we can exert— ought to be able to do a lot to remedy matters."

"As how?" Jim asked, really curious to know what Moran was approaching.

"You and I represent practically the whole of the county's business interests. We ought to have more of a say in running things than we have. As it is now—well, we haven't much of anything to say. Zaanan Frame says it all, and he's a stiff-backed, hard-headed old scoundrel if there ever was one. Talk about your city political bosses! Zaanan could show them things they won't be finding out for another twenty years."

"Pretty strong politically, is he?"

"Just this strong, Mr. Ashe, that he appoints the officers in this county. Appoints 'em. Of course there are elections, but if Zaanan told these farmers and what-not to vote for his horse Tiffany for President of the United States, that horse would come close to carrying the county unanimously. That's how strong he is. The circuit judge is his; the sheriff is his; the prosecutor is his. What chance has money in such a nest? The worst of it is, the old man's pretty well off and you can't reach him."

"Never can tell till you try," said Jim.

"I'm in a position to tell, all right. It's no go. The only thing is to get rid of him. If he could be beaten out of his own job I guess he'd be done for. And I think I can manage it with your help."

"I'm not aching to meddle with politics any."

"You will be when he hands you a dose of his medicine. Look at us. Probably a dozen little suits in the justice court every week come before him. What protection have we?" Moran spread his hands in a gesture of helplessness. "Any Tom, Dick, and Harry that wants to goes ahead and sues—and Zaanan sees to it we get the worst of it. Anywhere else we could appeal, but here the circuit court belongs to Zaanan, and it spends as much of its time playing to the gallery and coddling the poor, downtrodden working-man at my expense as Zaanan does."

"Pretty tough," said Jim. He told himself that here was first-class evidence to support the Widow Stickney's praise of Zaanan Frame. It was being admitted he was honest, that influence did not subvert justice. He was a boss, perhaps, but his virtues seemed to stamp themselves on the men his power put in office. Theoretically a boss is bad, Jim thought, but this case seemed to demonstrate there might be exceptions. Suppose Zaanan were absolute monarch of Diversity, what had made him so and what kept him in his place? Apparently it was the fairness, the rugged squareness, of the old man. Apparently he possessed the love and confidence of his people to the point that they were willing to delegate their powers to him in the belief that he would work better for them than they could for themselves.

"You bet," said Moran. "If we could get in a justice of the peace we could stop all these petty suits right there. Let a couple of dozen of these fellows find out they were going to get beaten, and the whole mess of them would quit. I hate to think how much money Frame costs me a year."

"Or how much he benefits the man who couldn't help himself without Zaanan's court," Jim thought. "It means much to the poor man to know that his court—the justice's court—is honest; that he can carry his wrong to it and see it righted! What's your idea?" he asked aloud.

"We'll have to get him in the caucus," said Moran. "Couldn't beat him at the election. I don't suppose there are a dozen votes cast against him in the whole county. But that's quite a while off. I just wanted to mention the matter to you and find out how you looked at it. I'm glad you agree with me."

"We can do more together than we could separately," Jim said, jesuitically.

The widow appeared in the doorway and announced supper. Jim waved Moran to precede him, and he walked to the table feeling more sure of his ground than he had been an hour before. His suspicions of Moran rested on a surer foundation—the man was not honest. He was the sort of business man who has brought stigma on his kind by bribery, by conniving at injustice, by seducing officers of justice. He was ruthless. The rights of others only represented something to be overridden. To Jim it seemed that the day when Michael Moran replaced Zaanan Frame as dictator of Diversity would be a black day indeed for the county.

Further, he made up his mind to win that friendship which Zaanan Frame had denied him. In his difficulty he felt a flood of gratitude to good fortune that such a man as Zaanan Frame was at hand and in power. When he took his seat at the table he was more cheerful than he had been for many a day; his face was lighter, his eyes brighter. The widow noticed his changed expression and was deeply curious to account for it. The widow was a motherly soul. Of late she had taken to coddling and worrying over Jim. Hers was a heart that could not be inactive—if man's persistent mortality discouraged her from taking another husband, she could, at least, secretly adopt a son.

CHAPTER XI

"Our school opens Monday, doesn't it, Marie?" asked Moran.

She turned her black eyes on him and allowed them to rest a moment before replying. Jim Ashe was aware of the somber glow of them.

"Yes," she said, shortly.

Moran chuckled. "You're tickled to death over it, aren't you?"

The glow of her eyes became a flame—such a flame as might eat its way through plates of steel. Jim Ashe would have drawn back from such a fire disconcerted; Moran was unable to meet it with his eyes, but he was not disconcerted. Instead, it seemed to give him satisfaction. He chuckled again.

"Well," he said, jovially, "you know you can leave it when you want to."

Jim was startled; looked quickly at Marie. The flame lay dead in her eyes; she seemed merely tired, very tired. Moran spoke again, this time to Ashe and the widow.

"I've offered her a place in my office back in town," he said. "I guess she don't hate Diversity as bad as she says she does, or she'd take it. But the offer holds good, Marie. Any time. Any time."

The widow ruffled her feathers.

"Marie's goin' to stay right where she is. Maybe Diversity hain't a suburb of heaven; maybe teachin' school's a long ways from strummin' a harp in Paradise; but Marie's got too much sense to go flutterin' off like a blind owl in the sunshine, not knowin' what she's like to bump her head against."

Marie turned slowly on the widow.

"When the time comes to choose I'll choose," she said, speaking, it seemed, not to the widow, but to herself.

The widow looked puzzled; even Moran seemed not to understand; but Jim understood. In the light of his first meeting with Marie on the knoll he comprehended the significance of her words, the rashness, the worldly wisdom of them. Hers would be no blindfold journey. If she spread her wings for flight it would be with eyes wide and seeing; it would be on a calculated course, and the cost would be itemized. He saw that she read Moran better than he had done, and in the light of her knowledge the page of Moran's soul became more legible to him. Before Moran had been an adversary--no chivalric adversary; now he felt a cold hatred for the man, a personal, throbbing hatred coupled with a stinging, physical aversion. From that moment Moran became a snake to be scotched.

"There's a lot less choosin' in this world than folks think there is," said the widow. "Folks spends a heap of time separatin' in their minds what they're goin' to do from what they hain't—gen'ally choosin' the pleasant and throwin' out the disagreeable. But when they git along toward the end of things and look back at the figgerin' they done, they mostly find that the good they chose wasn't the good they got, and the bad they chose not to have was the very thing that pestered them. Most folks meets up with about so much good and bad, about so much joy and so much trouble; but the joys hain't the ones they looked forward to and the troubles hain't the ones they feared."

Moran smiled and shook his head.

"I can't agree with you, Mrs. Stickney. We get what we plan for. Set your mind on a thing and then plan and wait and work toward it every chance you get. Don't give it up. Keep your mind on it. Don't let a chance slip to move nearer to it. What I want—if I want it bad enough—that thing I get."

Suddenly Marie spoke—to Jim.

"What's your opinion, Mr. Ashe?" she said.

"I? As old Sir Roger de Coverley said, 'There's much to be said on both sides.'" Jim had no desire to be drawn into argument with Moran.

Her lip curled. "We used to have a Congressman here who was called Midchannel Charlie because his attitude toward every question was like yours now. He was never Congressman but once."

"Well, then," said Jim, perceiving that for some reason she really desired his opinion, "I believe that if you don't choose and work to get the thing you have chosen, you miss one of life's finest games. I do agree with Mrs. Stickney that if you drift along and take what comes the chances are that good and ill will run a fairly even race. I agree with Mr. Moran that the man who visualizes his desire and sets it up before him as a lighthouse—and then rows his boat to it with all the strength of his oars—stands at least a moderate chance of getting there. But for me, I do not believe a man should be too set on a desire, that he should steer a course for his lighthouse regardless of everything else. If I have a plan of life it is to row for my lighthouse, but not to miss the scenery along the way. My boat may carry me past something better than my lighthouse. If I should suddenly find myself floating over an oyster-bed I should stop to hunt pearls. I believe that as a man pushes forward to his desire he should stand ready to pounce on the treasure that chance or circumstance floats in his way; he should be ready to repel the evil he fears, but he should keep his ammunition dry and his weapons loaded for trouble he doesn't in the least foresee—which is not likely to happen, but which sometimes does happen. I believe that a plan to arrive at one's choice should be modified by the happening of every moment, and that one should be ready to abandon his boat, abandon his lighthouse, to dive over the side after the chance-sent mass of floating ambergris."

"Yes. Yes, that's it. The moment determines. The mood of the moment determines," said Marie.

"And," said Jim, carried onward by the flow of his thought, "meetings with other voyagers determine. One's course is sure to cross the courses of others. At some point those moving at right angles to each other may meet bow to bow, when there will result collision, or else one or both the travelers must modify their courses for a time. It may even be that the adventure of one traveler will cause the other to abandon his quest and follow. If you're going to look ahead, Miss Ducharme, and plan and choose, you must not forget to estimate the chances of contact with other planners and choosers, nor the modifications contact may cause."

Moran shrugged his shoulders, his jaw set.

"If another man's path crosses mine, or his boat gets in the way of mine, I let him look out for himself or be run down," he said, crisply.

"In such collisions," said the widow, "I've knowed both boats to be sunk."

Jim felt Marie's black eyes upon him, but he did not look at her. She was studying him, appraising him. He was conscious of it, yet endeavored to appear unconscious. He felt she was more inclined toward friendliness with him than ever before, and because he perceived that she needed friendship—not because of any leaning toward her—he feared to show even by a glance that he was aware of a better understanding between them. It would be so easy to frighten her away.

Moran pushed back his chair.

"I must catch my train, Mrs. Stickney. I always enjoy my suppers with you. They remind me of suppers I used to eat at grandmother's farm."

"It's a good thing for men to git reminded of their grandmothers once in a while," she answered, cryptically.

"You're coming to see me to the door, Marie?" Moran said. It seemed to Jim more a command than a question. Marie obeyed, and the man and girl left the room.

Jim emptied his coffee-cup, which was not a thing to do quickly when the widow had made the coffee. Indeed not! One sipped and tasted and stopped betweenwhiles to think on the aroma of it. Presently Jim set down his empty cup.

"More?" asked the widow.

"Thank you, no."

Jim moved back his chair. He was frowning at the tablecloth abstractedly.

"Hum!" said the widow. It was a very significant, expressive hum, an eloquent hum, but, withal, a hum that needed further elucidation before it became wholly and perfectly clear.

"The difference between girls," she said, "is that most of them is just ordinarily foolish."

"And the difference between men," said Jim, "is that some of them are like Michael Moran."

"I calc'late from that," she said, "that your heart don't flow out to him in love and admiration."

"It's men like him that make murder a virtue."

"Hum!" said the widow. "I'll say this for you, you don't leave folks fumblin' round to understand your meanin'."

"I said exactly what I meant. Mrs. Stickney, Miss Ducharme is in a dangerous humor. I can't make her out. Probably it is because I'm too young. But you ought to understand her—whether she means some of the reckless things she says. I believe she does. She has intelligence and a will, which makes the condition more dangerous. She talks about choosing her course when Diversity becomes unbearable. Michael Moran is planning to be present when that time comes. Possibly his plans include making Diversity unbearable. At any rate, he plans and plans, and because he is what he is, because she knows he is what he is, he offers her an opportunity of escape. He offers her what she thinks is an opportunity to choose. But it won't be any such thing. When she chooses—if ever she does choose—to go to him, it will be because he has planned it and forced the choice."

"Hum!" said the widow again, eying him with eyes that age had not robbed of their brightness. "Hum!"

This was no startling contribution to the conversation. But the exclamation "Hum!" uttered by an old woman who has buried two husbands and kept boarders is not to be despised. There is more wisdom in such a monosyllable than in all the pages of the valedictory of a girl emerging from college—which is generally credited with being an erudite message. Two husbands and a succession of boarders may teach things that even professors of sociology have not had called to their attention.

"She's so infernally alone," said Jim.

Marie stepped into the dining-room again—one might almost say pounced. Her eyes glittered, her hands were clenched.

"I am infernally alone. Oh, I heard! I heard what you said before that, I listened. What business have you to discuss me and my affairs? I suppose it's your meddlesome notion to help me. I don't want help; I don't need help; and what help could you give? What do you know about me—or about life? What do you know about a woman? I will not be discussed by either of you. I have the right to order my own life—to make it good or bad as I want to—and it's nobody's business. Do you think I don't know Michael Moran? I tell you I see into the farthest corner of his soul. I'm not demanding happiness. I doubt if happiness is the best thing life has to give. But I do demand to live. Nobody can compel me to rot. What if I do suffer? What if there is pain and suffering and remorse? That is part of life. It is living. And you would meddle! I tell you again that I see what I am doing; that I am not deceived; that I have weighed consequences. If the time comes when Michael Moran is the stepping-stone I need, I shall use him. Nobody can prevent it—"

"I calc'late there's somebody might prevent it, Marie," said the widow, quietly, "and I calc'late there's somethin' would fill you up with a kind of regret you ain't anticipatin' if it was to happen afterward."

"Who?" demanded Marie, passionately. "And what?"

"The man you loved might stop you—and comin' to love a man afterward might bring that kind of remorse that would make dyin' better 'n livin'."

Marie stared at the widow, then after one might slowly have counted a dozen she sank into a chair and gazed fixedly downward. Nobody spoke, Jim felt extremely uncomfortable.

Presently Marie lifted her eyes, first to Jim, then to the widow.

"Yes," she said, "that is possible. I could love, but it would be better that I shouldn't. Better for him. If I loved it would be no pretty bill-and-coo. It would be love. I should give much, but demand much. I do not think it would be comfortable to be loved by me. If I loved it would be the one great concern of my life. I should have room for nothing else. I have studied myself. And if he did not love me as I loved him I should make him unhappy, for I do not believe men like to be bothered by too much love. I should make him hate me. I should be no sweet domestic animal to greet him with a kiss, and fetch him his slippers, and sit by placidly while he read his paper. Men like comfort and coddling. There would be no comfort with me. I should be jealous—jealous even of the food that gave him pleasure. What man wants such a love! What happiness can come from it? Would you want to be loved that way?" She turned abruptly to Jim.

"I do not believe one can love too much. I don't believe you know what love is, Miss Ducharme. If love is what I believe, it is not fierce, not a fire that burns beyond control. I think it is gentle; I think love forgives; I think real love manifests itself not by clawing and scratching its object, but by spending itself to procure his happiness—or her happiness. I believe the true love of a man for his wife, or of a woman for her husband, has much in it of the love of father or mother for their child. I do not think love threatens; it shelters. No, Miss Ducharme, the thing you have been talking about is not love at all. I don't know what it is, but love it is not."

She looked at him wide-eyed, startled, curious.

"When you love," he said, "you will see that I am right."

"I should like to believe you, Mr. Ashe," she said. "It would be sweet—sweet. But you are wrong. How could you know? Have you loved?"

"No."

Mrs. Stickney spoke, her old eyes twinkling.

"It don't seem scarcely possible," she said, "but I've been in love. It was some number of years ago, but I hain't forgot all about it yet. Shouldn't be s'prised if there was times when I remembered it right well. So I'm speakin' from experience. When I was in love 'twa'n't exactly like either one of them things you've been describin'. I'll go so far's to say that both of you'll know consid'able more about it after you've ketched it."

Jim felt a sense of relief. There had been a strain; the moments that had passed were tense moments. Possibly Marie, too, was relieved. At any rate, she stood up, and as she walked toward the door she spoke icily:

"Bear in mind, please, Mr. Ashe, that I and my affairs are not to be discussed, nor have you a right to interfere in whatever happens."

"Miss Ducharme, I have that right. If I see a man ill-treat a dog, I have the right to protect that dog—more than that, it is my duty. How much more is it a man's right and duty to interfere in behalf of a woman who is in danger!"

"Duty!" exclaimed Miss Ducharme.

CHAPTER XII

Jim found Zaanan Frame at his desk, Tiffany's *Justices' Guide* open before him as it always was in his moments of leisure. Zaanan nodded.

"Set," he said.

"Judge," said Jim, "I've been invited to help beat you at the next election."

"Um!"

"They tell me a corporation hasn't a chance with you."

"Some hain't," said Zaanan, briefly.

"And that a laboring-man gets all the best of it."

"An even chance is the best of it for a poor feller," said Zaanan. "Calc'late you was fetchin' me news?" The old man's eyes twinkled. "Moran's a convincin' talker," he observed, after a brief pause.

Jim made no reply.

"Thinkin' of throwin' in with him?" Zaanan asked.

Jim started to speak, but stopped, startled. It seemed to him for an instant that Marie Ducharme sat before him. He could see her move with the wonderful grace that was hers; he could see the sure, graceful lines of her figure; he could see her face, mobile, intelligent, with possibilities that would have made it interesting, even compelling, but for the expression of sullen discontent that masked it. So real, so material did she seem, that it seemed to Jim he could stretch out his hand and touch her. Then she was gone.

Jim's teeth clicked together, and his good, square-cornered jaw set.

"I'll tell you what I'm going to do," he said, with that sudden resolution which seemed to have become a part of him. "I'm going to chase Michael Moran out of Diversity County."

"Um! Hain't you perty busy savin' your own goods from the fire?"

"I'll keep mine and add something of his," Jim said, grimly.

"Wa-al, sich things has been done. Ever hear tell of Watt Peters and his bear? Watt he was campin' with a crowd back in the timber, huntin' bear. One day he was cruisin' round and come on to a old he-bear consid'rable more sudden than he calc'lated on. Watt he never got famous for boldness, so this time he clean forgot he was huntin' bear and turned and run for all was in him. Seems like he irritated that bear somehow, for he turned to and chased Watt 'most to camp. Watt he tripped over a root and like to busted his neck. Old bear he kept a-comin'. Wasn't anything for it but to shoot, so Watt he up and shot. Dummed if he didn't kill that there bear deader 'n a door-nail. Fellers in camp came a-runnin' out.

""'Most catched you, didn't he?' says a feller.

"'Catched me!' says Watt. 'What you mean, catched me?'

"'He was a-chasin' you, wasn't he?'

"Watt he looked scornful-like and answered right up:

"'Think I want to lug a bear two mile into camp?' says he. 'No, sir, I lured this here bear in so's I could kill him handy to where I wanted him. I jest figgered to make him carry himself into camp,' says he. Wa-al, young feller, things does happen that way sometimes, but it looks to me right now like the bear was chasin' you."

"I know Moran is in with Welliver and his bunch. I know Moran is at the bottom of the trouble we're having at the mill. He's having our logs spiked, and a man of his is tampering with our machinery. I know it, but I can't prove it even to myself. The first thing I do is to make certain."

"If I was goin' to take a drive," said Zaanan. "I'd take the River Road. Calc'late I'd drive till I come to where a beech and a maple's growin' so clost it looks like they come up from one root, and I'd up and hitch there. Then I'd walk off to the right, takin' care to make plenty of noise so's not to seem like I was sneakin'. About that election, Jim, I calc'late I'm obleeged to you. G'-by, Jim."

"Good-by, Judge," said Jim.

He went to the livery for a rig and presently was driving out the River Road according to Zaanan's directions. It seemed like a long time before he discovered Zaanan's landmark, but it appeared at last, and Jim was interested to see that another horse had been tied there not long ago. The marks of its pawing hoofs were visible in the soft soil; the work of its teeth showed on the bark of the tree. It was here that Dolf Springer had tied not many hours before.

Jim looked about him for some indication of man's presence that would show him how to proceed, but there was none. Away from him on all sides stretched a growth of scrub-oak and jack-pine, with here and there the grayed and splintered shaft of an ancient pine that had been riven by lightning or broken off by wind or age. There was no path, no sign of human usage.

Forgetting Zaanan's caution to proceed noisily, Jim walked slowly, almost stealthily, through the underbrush. He did so unconsciously; it was the natural impulse of one walking into the unknown. At times he stopped to look about him, dubious if he had not alighted at the wrong landmark.

Presently he fancied he heard voices and stopped to listen with straining ears. Unquestionably there were voices. Jim drew nearer softly, and in a few moments reached a point where words and tones and inflections could be distinguished. There was a man's voice and a child's voice. Jim stopped again and listened. The conversation he overheard was not a conversation; it was a ritual. As the words came to Jim he knew it was but one repetition of what had been conned and repeated many times before. Yet there was fire in it, fire and fierce determination.

"Where is your mother?" asked the man's voice.

"Dead," answered the child's.

"Who killed her?" asked the man.

"She killed herself," said the child.

"Why?"

"On account of me."

"Did she do right?"

"Yes."

"Who do you hate?"

"Michael Moran," said the child.

"What have you got to do?"

"Pay Michael Moran."

"You won't ever forget?"

"I won't ever forget," said the child.

"See to it that you don't," the man said, fiercely.

It was evident the ritual was at an end; that this last was an admonition, not a part of it. Jim shivered but he knew he had not gone astray, that here was the man Zaanan had sent him to see. He retired softly a hundred feet, then called aloud and floundered toward the spot where the ritual had been spoken.

Jim had not traversed half the distance before a man stepped from behind a mound. It was the same big, handsome, somber man whom Dolf Springer had called upon; it was Steve Gilders. Under his arm was the rifle that had sent a shiver up Dolf's spine.

"Lookin' for somebody?" he demanded.

"Yes. Judge Frame sent me."

"What's your name?"

"Ashe."

"Own the new mills down to Diversity?"

"Yes. Are you the man I came to see?"

"Calc'late so. Names is handy in talkin' to folks. Mine's Steve."

Jim thought it best not to ask additional names.

"What was you wantin'?" Steve asked.

"Somebody's playing hob with my machinery and driving spikes into my logs for me to rip off sawteeth on. I think Michael Moran is at the bottom of it, but I want to prove it to myself."

"If you kin prove it—what?"

"I'll have a better conscience to go after the man."

"Not after him personal. You won't lay hands on him? You hain't figgerin' on doin' anythin' to his body, be you? 'Cause I can't have that. That hain't your concern. It's a job for somebody else."

"No. But I'm going to drive him out of Diversity."

Steve smiled. "If you was to take his money away from him and his power away from him, why I'd be glad. It 'u'd hurt him mighty bad. But I calc'late he hain't goin' to be drove out of Diversity. I figger he's goin' to stay here permanent—permanent as them in Diversity's graveyard."

Jim wondered if the man were not off the mental perpendicular; but a glance at his fine if stern face, his clear eyes, his bearing, argued strongly in favor of his sanity. Perhaps the man was possessed of some Old Testament spirit of vengeance; perhaps here was a Northern relative of the blood feud of the Kentucky mountains. In spite of himself he felt apprehensive for Moran's sake.

"You want proofs, eh? Be you enured to walkin'?"

"I'll do my best," said Jim.

"Seven miles to the loggin'-road," said Steve.

"I'd better care for my horse then."

"I'll see to him. You set right where you be." It was a command. Jim recognized it as such and obeyed.

It was not long before Steve returned. He did not take Jim to his shanty as he had taken Dolf Springer, but led him straight through the woods toward the southeast. Steve tramped silently. The things his eyes saw, the things his ears heard, and the thoughts moving in his mind were company enough for him. As for Jim, he had difficulty enough maintaining the pace without wasting breath in unnecessary words.

After an hour's steady going Steve stopped suddenly.

"Set," he said. "You hain't used to this."

Jim sank down without a word. Steve leaned against a maple trunk, for they were now getting into the edge of the hardwood, and took out his pipe. Neither spoke for fifteen minutes. Then Steve straightened up and nodded. Jim got to his feet and followed.

In another hour Steve spoke again: "Road's right over there. First landin's half a mile up."

They turned to the left and shortly were in last season's slashings. Narrow lanes among the trees, uneven, impassable to teams at this season of the year, marked the tote roads, which in winter would be cared for more skilfully than many a city boulevard, iced, kept clear of refuse, so that heavily ladened sleds might pass smoothly, carrying logs from cutting to landings.

Jim heard the toot of a locomotive whistle and looked at his watch.

"Must be the empty trucks up from the mill," he said.

Steve nodded.

The engine with its trail of trucks passed them at their right, whistled again, and at last came to a stop. Jim knew the stop was at the landing from which came his logs.

"Where's the camp?" he asked.

"T'other side of the track."

In a moment they were at the edge of the clearing and Jim could see the landing, its skidways piled high with hardwood logs, beech, birch, maple, with here and there a soft maple, an ash or an oak. The train crew had already disappeared in the direction of the camp; only one man was visible, standing in the doorway of the sealer's shanty. He looked after the trainmen, then emerged and mounted a skid way. With a big blue crayon he marked log after log. These, Jim knew, were being selected to go to his mill in the morning. Then the man returned to his shanty.

Presently he appeared with a blacksmith's hammer. He mounted the skidway again, knelt upon a marked log, and drove a spike into it near the middle. This he proceeded to sink with a punch.

Steve did not so much as turn his head toward Jim. He merely watched the man with a curious intentness. The man repeated the operation five times on different logs, then returned his tools to the shanty and sauntered away toward the camp.

Jim felt a hot flame of rage. With characteristic impulse he started to his feet and would have demanded a reckoning of the man there and then, but Steve caught him by the arm and drew him down.

"Hungry?" he asked, in a matter-of-fact tone.

"Maybe I am," snapped Jim, "but I'm too mad to notice it."

"Spring back here. I put a snack in my pocket."

"What's that man's name, Steve?" Jim demanded.

"Kowterski—one of Moran's Polacks," said Steve, with bitterness in his voice. "Them cattle is drivin' good woodsmen out of the State. Moran's fetchin' 'em in 'cause he kin drive 'em and abuse 'em and rob 'em. There was a day when a lumberjack come out of the woods after the drive with his pockets burnin' with money. These fellers is lucky if they come out even. I knowed one that come out last spring with fifteen dollars to show for his winter's work. Sometimes Moran gives 'em half a dollar on Sundays—for church!" He stopped suddenly.

"Kowterski's brother's night-watchin' for you," he said, shortly.

"Thank you," said Jim. "Now let's go back."

"Better eat a bite," Steve said, and, taking Jim's assent for granted, led the way to the spring.

It was an hour before he consented to begin the backward tramp. It was completed as silently as had been the coming. Steve led Jim past his shanty, but not in sight of it, and to the road where the buggy stood.

"Wait," he said, and shortly reappeared, leading the horse, which he helped Jim to hitch.

Jim climbed to the seat and extended his hand. Steve made no movement to take it.

"I'm more obliged to you than I can say," Jim said.

"G'-by," Steve said, briefly, and, turning his back, strode out of sight among the scrub-oak and jack-pine.

The horse Jim drove was not intended by nature to travel rapidly from place to place. He possessed two paces, one a studious walk, the other a self-satisfied trot that was a negligible acceleration of movement. So it was dusk when Jim reached Diversity. Slow as the progress was, it did not give Jim time to cool down from the boiling-point he had reached; instead, it irritated him, brought him where explosion was inevitable.

He returned his horse to the barn and started down the street toward the mill, forgetful that he had eaten nothing but Steve's snack since breakfast. As he passed the hotel he saw Moran on the piazza—Moran, who had taken a train yesterday to the city.

Jim stopped, gripped his temper with both hands, as it were, to hold it in check, and spoke.

"You're back soon," he said.

"Didn't get to the city at all. Wire met me halfway and called me back."

"That's good," said Jim, with another of his sudden resolutions. "I'm glad you're here. Can you walk down to the mill with me? I want to show you something."

"Glad to," said Moran, rising.

The older man attempted casual talk as they went along, but Jim's answers were monosyllabic, even brusk. Moran studied the young man's face out of the corner of his eye, wondering what was in the wind. He was puzzled, uneasy, and he ceased his conversation and speculated on possibilities.

Jim led him round to the rear of the mill. At the fire-room door he paused and called, "Kowterski!"

Presently a bulky figure emerged from the gloom that was beyond the doorway. The man was big, with a clumsy bigness, not so tall as Jim, but heavier by fifty pounds. He came forward slowly.

"Here," said Jim. "Come here."

Kowterski recognized Jim and ducked his head.

"Evenin', boss," he said, then looked into Jim's face. Something he saw was disquieting, for he halted, took a step backward, started to raise his hands.

Putting the weight of his body into the blow, Jim struck him. Kowterski stumbled, went down. He lay still an instant where he had fallen, then wallowed to his knees and remained in that position, mumblingly ridding his mouth of blood and teeth.

"Git!" said Jim.

Kowterski rose, wavering, turned, and ran stumblingly away into the darkness.

Jim turned to Moran. "Good night," he said, shortly.

"You had something to show me," said Moran, thrown from his habitual poise.

"That was it," Jim said, and disappeared into the fire-room.

CHAPTER XIII

That night Jim patrolled the mill in the place of the watchman whose resignation he had accepted in front of the fire-room door. Through the long, dark hours he had time and quiet for reflection. His mind was stimulated by the occurrences of the day; he was aware of a clarity of vision, a straightness of thought, a satisfying concentration. His problem, in all its intricate difficulties, lay plain before him. He fancied he had read astutely his enemies' plans; his own plans began to take form.

Against Welliver and the Clothespin Club he would have to defend himself by business makeshifts and financial strategy. Them he did not underestimate nor did he exaggerate their menace. To defend himself against Moran his best course was to attack. It would now become his business to seek for a point of weakness, and there to deliver his first blow.

It was common talk that Moran was reaching out ambitiously. His former holdings had been considerable; now the affairs which he seemed to control were of magnitude. He had traveled from the one to the other in a short space, a space so short that Jim felt sure it had not been sufficient to multiply his fortune. It forced itself upon Jim that Moran must have spread himself out thinly to cover so much ground. In that case there must be a point where he had spread himself with dangerous thinness. That area, Jim thought, he must find. There, he said to himself, he must strike.

It was daylight when he left the mill and trudged wearily toward his bed at the widow's. On his way he met John Beam, who regarded him with amazement.

"Up kind of early, ain't you?" asked Beam.

"No, just a bit late to bed," Jim said, with a grin of boyishness. "By the way, you'll have to get a new watchman to take Kowterski's place. I took it last night."

"What's the matter with him?"

"When he left," said Jim, a trifle grimly, "I thought of advising him to go to the dentist's."

He looked down at his bruised, abrased knuckles. Beam's eyes followed his employer's and the man grinned with sudden comprehension.

"It was him, eh?" he asked.

Jim nodded. "I won't be down till afternoon."

Beam walked on his way, chuckling. Presently he encountered Nels Nelson and recounted what he had learned, with certain amendments and surmises of his own, ending with a special word regarding Jim.

"Some boss," he said, delightedly. "I've had a few bosses, but Sudden Jim he's the boy for my money." Which would have pleased Jim exceedingly had he overheard it.

Jim devoured the breakfast the widow had ready for him, and went off to bed. He went to sleep with the satisfying consciousness that it was now open warfare between him and Moran. What he had done last night was both a declaration of war and an eloquent expression of his opinion of the man. He knew Moran would be able to translate it correctly.

It was after one o'clock when Jim awoke, but he found the widow had kept his dinner warm for him.

"'S my experience," she said, severely, "that folks gits more for their money sleepin' nights than daytimes."

"I was behaving myself, Mrs. Stickney. Honestly I was. At regular rates I earned two dollars watching in the mill."

"I was kind of disap'inted in you when you didn't come home at all. But, 'Boys will be boys,' says I, 'which won't prevent my speakin' my mind to him if he hain't ready with a good excuse, which mostly young men is ready with and ain't usually believed; but what kin a body do about it?'"

"I hope you'll do nothing rash," Jim said, with specious soberness. "You won't put me out in the street, will you?"

"If it had been any of my husbands I'll bet I'd 'a' knowed the reason why," she said, and disappeared into the kitchen, with an aggrieved air.

Jim went out smiling; somehow the widow's threatened scolding put him in a better humor with the world. It was good to know that somebody in Diversity had a real, friendly, motherly interest in him.

His way led past Zaanan Frame's office. Zaanan was standing on the step.

"Afternoon," said the old justice. "Hain't much battered up as I kin see."

"I'm practically intact," Jim said, gaily.

"Folks round town has it there was consid'able trouble to the mill last night. You was reported laid up in bed with grievous injuries. Calc'lated I'd come round to see you."

"Nothing much. I just took Moran down to point out a circumstance to him."

"Moran? What's he got to do with it?"

"Why," said Jim, "I met him when I got back to town and invited him down to the mill with me. I—er—rid myself of Mr. Kowterski in his presence and left him to think it over. Haven't seen him since."

"He hain't got any misgivin's as to how you stand then, eh? You kind of rubbed his face in it, didn't you? Leetle bit abrupt, wasn't you?"

"If there's going to be a fight," said Jim, "I want it to be a fight. No sneaking under cover."

"Call to mind that British general—what's his name? Bradley—Bradish—some sich thing. Didn't pay no heed to a young feller named Washington when he was goin' to fight the Injuns. He come right out bold to fight like you're aimin' to do. But did the Injuns? Wa-al, accounts says not. They done consid'able sneaking and prowlin' under cover, and this general got all chawed up."

"I didn't want the man to think I was a fool."

"Um! Shows you're young, Jim. Hain't no better way of gittin' a strangle holt on to a feller than by lettin' him think you're a fool. The s'prise of findin' out sudden that you hain't comes nigh to chokin' him."

"Anyhow, it's done," said Jim.

"No argyin' that p'int. I notice Moran didn't leave town this mornin' like he calc'lated to. What you figgerin' on next? Looks like you run on to some facts up the River Road."

"I'm going to look for some more facts."

"What kind of facts, son?"

"Moran's got a thin spot. I want to find it."

"Um! Thin spot. Calc'late I understand you. Figger he's been spreadin' his butter so thin that the bread won't be covered enough somewheres, eh? Maybe so. Maybe so. Ever see a map of the Diversity Hardwood Company's holdin's?"

"No."

"I got one. Had the Register of Deeds fix it up for me, thinkin' it might come in handy."

Zaanan went to a cupboard and brought out a rolled map which he spread on the table. It was marked off in sections. Those owned by the company were blocked in with red ink.

"Nigh forty-five thousand acres," said Zaanan.

Jim bent over the map. The Diversity Company's property ran in two irregular, serrated strips. Between the two portions was a sort of strait nowhere marked with red.

"They're cut in two," said Jim. "Who owns the stuff between? Timbered, is it?"

"As good hardwood as ever growed. B'longs to old Louis Le Bar. Run between twenty and twenty-five thousand to the acre. And that's consid'able hardwood, son."

"Logically the company ought to own it."

"Logically it wants to, but old Louis won't sell. Anyhow, he wouldn't." Zaanan emphasized the last word significantly. Jim looked across the table into the old man's twinkling eyes, shrewd, kindly eyes belonging to a man who had learned humankind by scores of years of meeting with them in their adversities. Zaanan said no more, but rolled up his map.

"I take it," said Jim, "that you've shown me a fact. One of the kind I was looking for."

"Folks says Opportunity knocks on a feller's door," said Zaanan. "Maybe so, but more times it goes sneakin' past his house quiet in the dark. And sometimes it's hard to catch as a greased pig."

"Much obliged," Jim said. "Where will I find Le Bar?"

"Stiddy, now. Stiddy. Before you pick up that animile be sure it's a cat and not a skunk. You're one of them pouncin' kind of young men. This here's a time to study first and jump afterward."

Then an unusual thing happened. Dolf Springer burst in without knocking. He was excited, greatly excited, or he never would have ventured, for Zaanan's office was sacred.

"Judge," he panted, "what d'you think? They've up and done it. Didn't b'lieve they'd dast, but they did dast. They've up and announced Peleg Goodwin to run ag'in you for justice of the peace."

Zaanan eyed his henchman. "Git a breath, Dolf. Git a breath. Like's not you'll suffocate. Hum! Peleg, eh?" He turned to Jim. "Seem like old times," he said; "hain't had no opposition for the nomination in more 'n twenty year. Peleg Goodwin, deacon by perfession."

"I told you," said Jim.

Zaanan peered at him briefly and grunted.

"I hain't so young as I was wunst," he said. "Maybe my powers is flaggin'. Maybe this here is a spontaneous uprisin' of the folks, thinkin' maybe it's time I was put on the shelf. But, son, I don't hanker to go on no shelf—anyhow, not to make room for Peleg. But it was bound to come some day. Folks likes change, and I've been mighty permanent."

The old man leaned back in his chair and looked beyond Jim and Dolf; forgot them as his thoughts carried him back over the years. When he spoke it was not to them, it was to the people, to his people, whom he had served and ruled for more than a quarter of a century.

"Yes, folks," says he, "what some of you is sayin' is correct. I calc'late I'm a boss. But if you was to look at my bank account or search out my property you'd see I wasn't that kind of a boss. I've run things in this county 'cause I was more fitted to run 'em than you. I'd have liked it if you'd 'a' had the spunk and gumption to run things yourselves. I've let you try it sometimes, and then had to clean up the mess.

"Don't think, folks, that all these years has been pleasure for me, nor what I'd 'a' picked out to do. No, siree! When I was younger there was things I had ambitions about. I wanted to git somewheres and be somethin'. But I hain't had no time. I hain't had no time to spare to look after Zaanan Frame, owin' to matters of yourn that was always pressin'. Diversity wa'n't no heaven when I took holt of it, but now it's a good place for man to live. I've made the laws respected and obeyed; since I've been justice one man's had as much chance in this county as another.

"The days and nights I might 'a' spent buildin' up Zaanan Frame I've spent buildin' up you. But I guess you're tired of it. If it was a good man and a true man and a man worthy of trust I calc'late I could step out of the way. There's times when I git mighty tired. But not for Peleg. Dolf," he said, sharply, "I guess we'll have to show Peleg and the feller that's puttin' him up to this some real politics."

"You bet!" said Dolf.

"It's Moran," Jim said; but the statement was half a question.

"He's the citizen," said Zaanan.

"They'll try to get you in the caucus."

Zaanan nodded. "Dolf," said he, "if you was goin' out to talk about this, what would you be sayin'?"

"That we was goin' to roll up our sleeves and lick the pants off'n 'em," said Dolf, belligerently.

"Don't calc'late you'd say I was perty hard hit? Eh? Sort of insinuate the blow bore down on my threescore and ten year? Nor that there didn't seem to be scarcely any fight left in me?"

"Dummed if I—" began Dolf. Then he stopped and looked at Zaanan. "Guess maybe that's about what I'd say," he responded, presently.

"G'-by, Dolf," said Zaanan.

"G'-by, Judge," said Dolf.

"Tain't only me," said Zaanan, after a time, "it's the sheriff and the prosecutor and the circuit judge—the whole kit and b'ilin' of us. There won't be a decent official left in the county. Law and justice'll be bought and sold and traded in like so much farm produce."

"I want to help if I can," said Jim.

"Calc'late I'll need what help I kin git. Moran don't usually start a job he can't see his way to finish. I'll call on you when you're needed. Louis Le Bar lives four mile to the west. How's things at the widder's? Do consid'able cacklin' over you, does she?" He stopped and scratched his head and appeared to ponder. "Say, young feller," he said, in a few moments, "what's your special grudge ag'in Moran? Tain't jest his business dealin's with you. It's him you want to git at, ree-gardless. What's he done to you?"

"There's a girl up at Mrs. Stickney's—" Jim began, slowly.

"Um!" grunted Zaanan, and his eyes twinkled. "Moran hain't in no position to cut you out with a girl. He's got more wife 'n he knows what to do with now."

Jim felt himself flushing. He had not connected Marie Ducharme with himself in the way Zaanan connected her. He had not considered his hatred of Moran as prompted by jealousy, nor had he looked on Moran as a rival. It was a new idea to him. He considered it. What interest had he in Marie? Did he even like her? He had fancied he disliked her for her sullenness, her rashness, for the bitterness of her temper toward the world. She was all somber shadows or lurid flame; there was no rosiness of dawn, no brightness of noontime, no peaceful, pure light as of the stars.

When Jim had thought of the woman who was to share his life he had pictured her as bright with star-brightness. He would stand something in awe of her, yet her brightness would not be cold, aloof—not cold moon rays. It would be tender, glowing, throbbing, but, above all, pure, inspiringly pure. Marie knew evil. Her discontent had seen its beckoning finger; she had felt the persuasive touch of its hand on her arm—and had not fled in horror. She eyed it cynically, plumbing its possibilities. Jim's girl would have felt herself indelibly smirched by thoughts that Marie gave willing housing to. Withal, what did he think of her? What was his interest in her? He could not answer. He dared not answer himself, for he found himself contemplating her with fascination. There was an appeal to her. Her possibilities were magnificent. He found himself wishing for her presence, for the sight of her movements of grace, the sound of her voice, the vivid life desire that lay in her eyes.

"Moran takes her to the top of a high mountain and shows her the kingdoms of the world," he said, in a hard voice. "He offers them to her."

"And you're afraid she'll accept?"

"She hates Diversity; life discontents her. She is bored. Moran plans deliberately, adds lure to lure. If he catches her in the mood—"

"Interestin' girl, eh? Talk intelligent? Good company?"

"She can be if she chooses."

"Ever try to git her to choose?"

"She doesn't like me."

"Huh! Hain't much in the way of excitement in Diversity, but pleasure's where you look for it hard enough. I call to mind enjoyin' buggy rides. Ever try to make things pleasant for Marie?"

"No." Jim said it with a guilty feeling.

"My experience," said Zaanan, "is that the run of girls prefers a decent, entertainin' young man to a bad old one. In gen'ral my notion is folks'd rather be good than bad, rather pick out right than wrong. Buggy hire don't come expensive." The old fellow eyed Jim with a twinkle.

Jim returned Zaanan's look; comprehension came to him.

"Judge Frame," he demanded, "did you send me to Mrs. Stickney's because Marie Ducharme was there?" The twinkle in his eye answered Zaanan's. "Was I just a checker you were moving in your game?"

"It's my policy," said Zaanan, "to git as many young checkers as I could moved safe into the king row of marriage."

"But she dislikes me."

"Hain't heard you say you was prejudiced ag'in her. Ever ask her if she disliked you? Um! Better try a few buggy rides first. Kin you drive with one hand?"

"I believe," said Jim, "you'd try to regulate the sex of Diversity's babies."

"If I calc'lated it'd benefit the town I dun'no' but I'd kind of look into the matter. G'-by, Jim!"

CHAPTER XIV

As the days went by Jim Ashe acquired a marked aversion to the upper right-hand drawer of his desk. For it contained the unpaid bills of the Ashe Clothespin Company. When Jim came the drawer had been empty; now it looked as if he would have to add an annex to care for the overflow. There were supply bills, machinery bills, stock bills. And Jim did not dare to pay them, for his account at the bank was running perilously low. Bills may be put off, but the pay-roll must be met on the minute.

From nothing the unsecured indebtedness climbed to five thousand, to ten thousand dollars. Much as it grieved Jim to see discount days pass with discounts not taken, it grieved Grierson more. He had served the company for many years. Never before in his experience had it failed to discount its bills—and to a bookkeeper of Grierson's type discounts are sacred. Grierson's type of mind would borrow money at six per cent. to take a two-per-cent. discount.

Finally statements began to arrive, some accompanied by letters setting forth in the polite verbiage of the business world that the creditor would be glad to have the company's check "for this small amount at its convenience." Dunning letters! Grierson was shocked. He blushed as he bent over his ledgers. The Ashe Clothespin Company had to be dunned as if it were a dubious individual with an overlarge bill at the corner grocery.

Jim was not yet the complete business man, but he did discover that certain larger creditors were willing to accept notes for the time, notes bearing interest at six per cent. Somehow it relieved his anxiety to issue this paper. At any rate, it postponed the day of reckoning in each case for three or four months. But Grierson was bitterly ashamed. He regarded it as such a makeshift as an unstable enterprise would avail itself of to ward off insolvency. Jim caught the old bookkeeper looking at him accusingly. Such things had never come to pass in his father's day.

Yet these were the very things Clothespin Jimmy had predicted. He had told Jim there would be sleepless nights and anxious days; he had confessed to milking the business. Now Jim appreciated what his father meant. With the fifty thousand dollars which Clothespin Jimmy had subtracted from the assets the company would be as sound as the Bank of England.

What worried Jim more than the accumulation of bills was the failure to make shipments as rapidly as the necessities required. Where he should have shipped a car-load a day he had been able to bill out an average of less than four cars a week. Customers clamored to have their orders filled;

cancellations were threatened; yet the mill failed to produce as it should produce. Somewhere something was wrong. Clothespin-machines that ought to have made their eighty five-gross boxes a day did not climb above sixty. Total shipments that should have amounted to thirty thousand dollars a month faltered and failed at fifteen or sixteen thousand. In short, he was spending every week a great deal more money than he was earning.

Much of this, he knew, was due to breakdowns caused by Kowterski; some of it to poor timber; some to timber spiked by Kowterski's brother. But aside from that, changes had to be made in machines; the mill did not run smoothly. Where construction should have ceased to lay its expense on the company it continued to demand its thousands of dollars every month.

But Kowterski was gone. Jim did not believe Moran would venture to send down more spiked timber. The mill was slowly but surely rising to a point of efficiency. Jim was confident in it; he placed full dependence on Nels Nelson, his millwright, on Beam, his superintendent. He knew they were doing their intelligent best and that their worries stood shoulder to shoulder with his own. Given time, he would be firm on his feet; given capital to carry him through this dubious period, and the company would pay bigger dividends, reach a more stable credit than it had ever before enjoyed. But the time and the capital!

In his heart he knew that if one creditor lost faith and brought pressure to bear, the whole edifice would come down in ruin. Construction, rebuilding, repairs, had devoured the money that should have paid bills. Bills had multiplied by reason of supplies necessary for construction. One thing was essential—construction must cease. Men employed in construction must be laid off.

"Grierson," he said, "make me a statement of our condition—a full statement; one that will show everything and show it truly. I'm going to see if there isn't somebody in the world who will appreciate being told the whole uncolored truth."

With this statement in his pocket Jim went to the city to its largest bank.

"I'm Ashe, of the Ashe Clothespin Company up at Diversity," he told the president, "and I'm in a hole. I've got to have some money."

"We've got lots of it," the president said, genially, "if you can show us. Let's look into the hole you're in and see."

Jim gave him the statement; it was fully, minutely itemized. Every debit was shown in full; no credit was inflated. The banker studied it half an hour, nodding now and then.

"Would you attach your name to that statement?" he asked.

"Yes," said Jim.

"You believe you can make money?"

"I know it."

"Show me," said the banker, and Jim showed him for an hour. He gave production figures, costs, prices, profits.

"It's a good statement, a sound statement," the banker said. "You have no quick assets—that's bad. That demand-paper I don't like; but otherwise—otherwise it is a very creditable statement."

Jim was astonished.

"How much do you want?" the banker asked.

"Twenty-five thousand dollars," Jim said, hesitatingly.

"I guess we can fix that up. The board meets at noon. Can you come in and tell them your story?"

"Certainly."

"You believe twenty-five thousand dollars will bring your mill to efficiency and carry you to a point where your own sales will take care of expenses?"

"I'm sure of it."

"Come in at twelve, then, and we'll see."

Jim returned at twelve and repeated his facts to the assembled board. Before they broke up Jim had given them the company's note for twenty-five thousand dollars, had that amount on deposit in the bank, and a book of blank checks under his arm.

"We've passed this loan," said a white-haired old gentleman, "because we like the moral risk. Your statement was fair; what you have said to us was spoken as an honest man speaks. You seem to have gotten a dollar of value for every dollar you have put into this mill, and we hope you'll win out. We believe you will or we wouldn't be lending you our money. You haven't evaded a question; you haven't held anything back. You've confessed to us that you thought you were in a bad hole, which is a poor argument for a borrower to bring forward. Maybe we'd have lent you on the security of the mills; maybe not. What we've done is to lend it on the security of you. I say this to you because it must give you pleasure to hear it and because it gives me pleasure to be able to say it. I cannot say such things as often as I wish. Now go to it, young man, and lick the stuffing out of that other crowd."

Jim went out, his head in a pink cloud, his feet treading something lighter than mundane pavement. Why, they had not thought he was in a hole at all!

The things Grierson and he had looked on as scarcely creditable makeshifts were approved as sound business, and they had given him money. How easy money was to get! It astonished him. Thirty thousand dollars he had borrowed from the Diversity Bank, with no difficulty; twenty-five thousand more poured into his purse from the City Bank, with compliments attached. His policy had won. He had found some one who appreciated being told the whole uncolored truth. After all, the world had not trampled its ideals into the mire of money-chasing. Even to-day the sound things of life commanded a market value. Business men, in high places of trust, business men of tested capacity, placed the moral before the material risk.

The president of the bank had said, "I would rather lend a known honorable man money on doubtful security than to venture a loan to a dubious man on Government bonds."

So Jim brought back from the city more than money. He brought back a renewed, an increased faith in the virtue of mankind. It was an asset not to be despised. The mighty hand of business reached out to encourage, to help with concrete aid, the honest man. It withheld its support, even though ample security were offered, from the man whose honor was dubious. Therefore, this modern god of business was a virtuous god. If evil were committed in its name the god itself was not smirched save in the eyes of the ignorant; if false sacrifices were offered to it by charlatans and liars and cheats, by jack priests of commerce, the god was not more dishonored than is the God of Israel by horrors that have been committed in His name.

As Jim rode home on the train his first feeling of elation dwindled. Doubt returned. He weighed the sides of his ledger against each other and determined all was not yet secure. How could it be secure when he had but added to his liability the not inconsiderable sum of twenty-five thousand dollars? Part of his debts he could pay. The balance must wait, for he could not divest himself of ready money, nor would the reserve he could set aside last forever.

The demand-note of thirty thousand dollars reared itself as a threat, assumed the guise of a poised bird of prey biding its moment. No, he was not free from the chains of his difficulties. His competitors—he thought of them as enemies—were as yet strong, untouched, unready for peace. They were capable of striking, would strike if a telling blow could be launched. There was Michael Moran.

The task of defending his own was just begun; the feat of bringing his enemies to overtures of peace was distant from accomplishment; and again there was Michael Moran. It was Jim's first contact with that black spirit called hatred. He hated Michael Moran because it was inevitable he should do so, because Michael Moran was the exponent of all things at the remotest pole from Jim's ideals.

With something like consternation he admitted to himself that he hated Michael Moran because the man's life orbit had touched with pitch the life of a woman who had assumed preponderating importance in Jim's universe.

As he alighted from the train at Diversity he saw Marie Ducharme as he had first seen her weeks ago. She stood motionless, a statue with lines of loveliness surmounted by a face of hopeless discontent. In her eyes was the look of hunger, like that of the starving woman in the bread-line. She gazed after the departing train as one might gaze after a hope dispelled.

Jim walked toward her. She saw him and nodded coolly.

"School's out early," he said.

"It's Saturday," she replied, shortly.

She turned away from the depot, no cordiality in her manner, but Jim was not to be rebuffed. He kept at her side.

"Since I have been here," he said, "I have never driven out along the lake shore. They tell me it is a beautiful drive."

"Yes," she replied, without interest.

"The train was warm, the dust got into my throat. Seems as if I were filled with it. All the way I kept thinking of expanses of clean water and of breezes off the lake. Won't you extend our truce to a drive out there with me this evening?"

She turned to him with a queer, abrupt, birdlike, startled movement. There was no pretense about it, she was surprised, jolted so that one peeped for an instant through her mask of sullenness to the loneliness, the yearning within. The crack closed instantly.

"Why do you ask me?" she demanded. "You don't like me."

"I asked you because I want very much to have you go. And I do not dislike you."

"Everybody does."

"I can't speak for everybody, but I doubt it. You—you have a way of shouldering folks off, of retiring behind the barbed wire. Folks would be willing enough to like you if you'd let them."

She pondered this and shook her head slightly.

"Part of what you say is true. There aren't many people here I want to like me. Haven't you lived here long enough to see that the people who stay here are the culls, the weak ones? Is there a young man or a young woman here with gumption? Just as soon as a boy amounts to a row of pins, gets an education or has ambition, he goes away. It is the same with the girls. The desirable go, the other sort stay. This is a backwater of life with nothing in it but human driftwood."

Jim appreciated the insight of her words. She spoke with some exaggeration, but with more sound truth. Her words might be a true arraignment of the average small town, secluded, with insufficient outlet or inlet. They might apply to a thousand villages in Michigan, in Vermont, in New York, in Tennessee. He understood her better than ever before—indeed, here was his first step in comprehension.

"You're lonesome," he said, more to himself than to her.

"Yes," she said, simply. "Lonesome—and bored, horribly bored."

"I am lonesome, too. Lonesome, but not bored. I have too much on my mind to be bored, which is better for me, probably. So won't you mend my lonesomeness for one evening by driving with me?"

"If you will say on your honor that you want me to," she said.

Jim listened for a note of wistfulness in her voice; fancied he distinguished it; was not certain he did.

"On my honor," he said, half-laughingly, "I do want you." Then, "Might we not ask Mrs. Stickney to put up a lunch for us and start right away?"

Again she looked at him, for there had been a note of boyish eagerness in his voice, and she smiled a very little. The smile was a revelation; while it lasted her face was not the face of a discontented woman, versed in the unpleasant things of the world, but of a girl, an eager, wistful girl.

"I should like it," she said.

How was Jim to know this was an event in Marie Ducharme's life? How was he to know it was her first social invitation from a man whom she cared to have as a companion, who was fitted by intelligence, by ideals, to be her companion? How was he to know that she had never driven with a young man as other country girls drive with neighboring boys? She was excited. Something welled up inside her that made breathing difficult, but that was delightful.

Jim, too, was young. His experience had not taught him how hard is the problem of the girl in the village—how marriage looms before her as the sole end to be desired, and how difficult is a suitable marriage to attain. He did not know how many girls with brains, with ideals, with ambitions, have, to escape spinsterhood and its dreariness, allowed themselves to be married to bumpkins, whose sole recommendation was their ability to provide support. Nor did he know how many such girls wore out their souls and their hearts in bitterness through lengthening years. Such a fate Marie Ducharme was determined to escape.

CHAPTER XV

Jim and Marie Ducharme took the north road out of Diversity. There were eyes that saw them and tongues that wagged when they were gone. Many supper-tables were supplied with a topic of conversation that had been barren without.

"Some day," said Jim, "I'm going to have a farm, and raise red pigs and black cows and white chickens."

"Horrors!" exclaimed Marie; but there was just a note of playfulness in her voice, the first Jim ever had heard there. "Some day I'm going to have an apartment in a hotel, where there's a Hungarian orchestra at dinner, and servants to answer pushbuttons, and taxicabs in front that take you to theaters. And I'm going to raise—well, not pigs and cows and chickens."

"I shall come in off my farm twice a year to eat with you while the orchestra plays and the pushbuttons buzz and the taxicabs click off exorbitant miles on their meters as we go to those theaters. Pigs and cows and chickens wear, they're durable company; the other thing is too heady for me. Like champagne once in a while. But one prefers water as a steady diet."

"I've only read about champagne," she said, the sullen mask dropping across her face for an instant.

"I'm going to have my farm near the lake," he said, "so I can lie with my back against a tree and watch it. It is a hundred different lakes every day, and I'd like to get acquainted with all of them."

"And I'd like to be aboard the most palatial steamer that floats, and ride past you, on my way to great cities."

"I'd be happiest," he said.

"I'd be—most excited," she replied.

"The most pitifully bored faces in the world are to be seen in Broadway cafes after midnight."

"But don't you like to be where things are flashing? Where life is moving so fast you can hardly follow it? Doesn't it spell happiness for you to be where a new thrill is always at hand for the asking?"

"That sort of thing is bully for dessert, but I want it after a long, satisfying meal of quiet contentment."

"Such as you have in Diversity?"

"Such as can be had in Diversity," he replied.

"What makes contentment? I should like to have it."

"Contentment," he said, slowly, selecting his words cautiously, "means to me the quiet feeling of decency and satisfaction and restfulness that comes to a man who is busy with a worth-while job. To have it fully there must be a home, a real home with a wife in it, and lads, and a dog and cat. All of them must be glad to see you come home at night, and sorry to see you leave in the morning. To have it your wife must believe in you more than you deserve, and you must trust her, and confide in her, and advise with her on all your concerns, sure of her interest. Yes, I think that is the indispensable element—marriage. The right sort of marriage—the sort the majority of folks are blessed with."

"It all sounds rather tame," she said. "Marriage. Must I marry to be contented?"

"To be so perfectly."

She laughed shortly. "I shall depend on a steady routine of excitement to make me forget I'm not contented," she said. "Marriage!" She spoke almost savagely. "Of course marriage is the solution of everything. Women are taught to look forward to it from the cradle as—as their means of support. We're trained to please men; we're dressed to attract men; our whole lives are aimed at men. We catch one at twenty or at twenty-five, and our career is over. We've succeeded in life. Then we live on till sixty."

"You've read only the introduction to the story," he said, soberly. "The book doesn't begin to get interesting until you pass that."

"Very well, then. I must marry to be contented. But whom? Diversity isn't swarming with husbands of any sort. Among the few available male inhabitants, how many would you pick out as welcome husbands for a girl with ambitions above turnips and the number of eggs a day? If you were a girl, with reasonable intelligence, reasonable capabilities to appreciate what we consider it cultured to appreciate, what man here would you pick out from Diversity's young men who wouldn't be a constant horror to you?"

"You're not limited to Diversity."

"But that is exactly what I am."

There was no obvious answer to this, and Jim drove on in silence. He sensed something of the girl's position; appreciated, as he had not before appreciated, the feeling almost of despair that came over her as she looked into the future and found it gray, without gleaming lights or frightening shadows. She was a bird imprisoned among frogs.

Presently they came to a little bridge over a stream which added its little flow to the volume of the lake. It was one of those reed-bordered streams which travel with a soothing lilt, winding along leisurely, contentedly.

It was not such a boisterous stream as the speckled trout loves; it was the sort where tiny turtles sun themselves on root or log, to slide off with a startled splash as you approach. Cows would have loved to wade in it of a hot day.

"Wouldn't you rather be a stream like that," Jim asked, "than to go plunging and leaping and bruising yourself down the rocks of a mountainside?"

She smiled, but did not answer. The picture had soothed her; it lay gently on her spirit, softening her mood.

"There's a cat-boat," Jim exclaimed. "Wonder if we can't borrow it. It'll be just a cat-boat to me, but you can turn it into your palatial steamer, if you want to. Shall we try?"

"I'd love it," she said. "I have never sailed."

Never sailed! Yet she had spent her whole life in sight of Lake Michigan.

"Then," said Jim, "you'll sail now if I have to turn pirate and steal us a craft."

But the transaction went smoothly. The little boat was rented, the horse unharnessed and stabled; they embarked their provisions, and with a brisk sailing breeze headed out for distant, invisible Wisconsin.

Jim handled sheet and tiller; Marie half reclined at his side. And because she was happy, for the hour she seemed beautiful to him—she was beautiful. Jim felt the force of her, not exerted in futile rebellion, wasted, but to be reclaimed by a wise hand and directed to the great work which falls to the lot of all good women. He saw her superior in mind to the women he knew; quickened by ambition. He saw her as she might be, indeed as she was at the moment. Her appeal was powerful. He compared her with women he had known; she made them seem faded, colorless. He glanced at her; his glance became a scrutiny of which she was unconscious. She seemed very desirable to him. It came over him suddenly that he must have her; that she was the necessary woman. It was as if he had known it always.

It was Sudden Jim who spoke.

"Marie," he said, and at the sound of his voice, the tremor in it, she turned, startled. "Marie," he repeated. No other word came for a moment, but his face, his eyes, were eloquent. The color left her face, left her lips first. "Marie, won't you be a part of that contentment? Won't you help me to it—and let me help you to it? I want you. I—love you, Marie. I want the right to love you always—and to take care of you and make you happy. I want you to love me."

She sat stiffly erect, unbelief in her eyes. Her hands gripped each other in her lap. She was amazed; not frightened, but something akin to it.

"I want you to let me try to make you smile, always, as you have smiled once to-day. I want to make the world sing for you, so that you will love the world, too. I want to take that look, that hunger look, out of your eyes forever, and put something else in its place. I want every act of mine, as long as I shall live, to add something to your happiness. You! You! Just you!" He held the sheet and tiller with one hand, stretched the other to touch her fingers gently.

"Marie, can't you—won't you—take me into your life? Will you marry me—very soon?"

"Marry you!" she said, in a whisper.

She looked about her as if searching for a way of escape. Then she stood up abruptly and ran forward to the very peak of the little craft, and crouched there on her knees, her chin in her hands, her eyes closed, or opening to peer off across the reaches of the lake. Jim could see her shiver now and again as though a chill wind blew over her. She did not speak.

After a time he called to her.

"Marie, I did not mean to frighten you. I—I was abrupt—"

"You did not frighten me," she said.

He plucked up heart. "I can't come to you," he said, yearningly. "I can't talk to you so far away. Won't you come back to me?"

She shook her head. "Not now," she said. "I—Oh, let me think. Let me be quiet."

He was patient. That much wisdom was given him in this hour. It grew dusk. Jim could only see the dark huddle of her body beyond the mast. It stirred. She was at his side again.

"You don't love me. You can't love me. I am not lovable, I know."

"Your word shall be my law—except for this one time. I do love you."

"No! No! It is pity, sympathy, something. I told you once what love would be if it came to me. It would be no gentle thing. It would make you hate me. You do not want my love."

"It is the one thing I want."

"I mustn't," she whispered to herself. "I mustn't." Then to Jim: "I don't love you. You would repent it if you had made me love you. While I was up there"—she pointed to the bow—"I thought of marrying you—to escape from Diversity. Yes, I thought of that—without love. But it would be no escape. You are tied to Diversity. It would be the same as before. I hate Diversity. It smothers me. If I loved you I wouldn't marry you. Diversity would stand between us."

Jim sat quietly. He had no hope on which to base expectation of any other answer. How could she love him? He had not tried to win her love; had pounced suddenly with talk of love.

"How could you love me?" he said, repeating his thought. "But won't you let me work for your love? I should try to earn it. If love came you would forget that Diversity was hateful to you. It would be a garden to you as it is to me—for my love had blossomed there."

"No," she said, sharply. "If I worshiped you, and you asked me to live in that miserable town, with its miserable people, I should refuse. It would torture me, but I could not live there."

"Think," he urged. "Take time to think. This has come to you unexpectedly. Wait before you set your will against my love. Give me my chance."

"No. You must not speak of it again. I am only an incident in your life. Set me aside. Forget this afternoon. You must forget it."

"You won't consider? You won't wait for another day's judgment?"

"No."

Jim turned away his face, turned it away from her lest the embers of the sunset should show how gray, how tired, how discouraged it was.

"I—I'm sorry," she said, softly.

He turned and smiled. "I am glad," he said. "Glad I love you, no matter what comes between now and the end. I shall not worry you again with it, but I want you to know, to be sure in your heart, day by day, every hour, that I do love you and am longing for you. I have spoiled your evening."

"No," she said. "It has been—sweet. So sweet!"

He was startled to see her burst into tears, and sob with great, wrenching sobs that shook her small body.

Presently she became calm, dried her eyes, smiled, and her smile was the ghost of a spirit of wistfulness.

"If only," she said, tremulously, "I were like other girls. But I'm not. I'm me. I'm selfish. I despise myself."

"No, no," he said; "don't remember this with a thought of pain. And do not withdraw from me altogether. Let us cancel to-night to start to-morrow on a new basis—as friends. You are lonely; I am lonely. I'll not worry you with love. But I'll try to be a dependable friend to you. Can we do that?"

"It sounds impossible," she said, "but we can try."

Love finds encouragement in trifles. The weight of Jim's heaviness became less. He hoped. If Pandora had not loosed hope into the world the lovers' portion would be miserable indeed.

It was late when they reached the Widow Stickney's, but she was waiting for them in her parlor. Her old eyes with their years of seeing were not to be deceived. She saw what she saw.

Marie went quickly to her room. They said good night at the foot of the stairs. Jim extended his hand, held her little one in his grasp.

"Good night, friend," he said, and smiled into her face.

She sat beside her window without undressing, motionless, even her eyes seeming without motion. She was wrestling, even as Jacob had wrestled, with an angel. But her angel had no divine touch of the finger to conquer her as the patriarch had been conquered.

The angel met defeat.

Marie lay face downward on the bed, tearless, passing through the agony she had brought on herself.

"I love him," she whispered. "I love him. But I can't. I can't."

CHAPTER XVI

Between the fall of darkness Sunday night and the breaking of dawn on Monday industrious persons had beautified Diversity by nailing to tree, fence, and barn half-tone productions of a photograph of Peleg Goodwin, wherein Peleg was shown wearing a collar of the Daniel Webster type and an expression like a slightly soured Signer of the Declaration. Peleg's beard was neatly trimmed; there was a part in his bushy hair. Somehow it did not impress one as authentic, but as a bit of trick photography. It excited some argument. People were disinclined to believe it really was Peleg, but some more glorious being who chanced to resemble Peleg somewhat.

"That there Peleg!" snorted Dolf Springer. "You couldn't pound Peleg's face into no such noble expression with a sledge. That there's Peleg's twin brother that died and went to heaven 'fore Peleg got him into bad habits."

"If that's Peleg," said old man Ruggles in a voice like a wheezy tin whistle, "then these here blue jeans is broadcloth weddin'-pants."

"I don't see but what it resembles him close," said a supporter of Goodwin's.

"That," said Dolf, "is prob'ly 'cause somebody's give you a dollar to think that way."

"My vote hain't for sale," shouted the virtuous citizen.

"Neither does a mortgage draw int'rest," said Dolf.

Jim drove on, chuckling. One thing was apparent—somebody was spending money to defeat Zaanan Frame. It was not all going for printing, either, Jim felt certain. How would Zaanan meet this attack? Had he money to spend in a campaign? A worry lest the old fellow had passed his fighting-day oppressed Jim. He stopped at Zaanan's office.

"I see the campaign has opened," he said.

"Peleg's a handsome critter, hain't he?" Zaanan said.

"Moran's going to dump a lot of money and a lot of dirty politics in here," Jim said. "What are you going to do about it?"

"Me? Not much, I calc'late. I hain't what you'd call a political campaigner. Don't go in for no hip-hurrah just 'round election-time. Keep reasonable busy the whole twelve months."

"Aren't you going to do anything to offset Moran's money?"

"Dun'no's I be," said Zaanan, placidly.

"They'll beat you in the caucus as sure as you're a foot high," Jim said, anxiously. "They've got to do it there. I don't believe they could worry you in an election."

"Caucuses is uncertain," said Zaanan. "Delegates and sheep is close related. Can't never tell when or where they'll run."

"Do you need money?" Jim asked, a shade diffidently. "I thought if you did—"

"Young feller, if I had a million dollars I wouldn't spend a cent. If folks elect me to office it'll be 'cause they want me, and not 'cause they're paid to vote for me. But I calc'late I'm obleeged to you. It was a right friendly offer."

"Is there anything I can do?"

"Yes," said Zaanan, with a chuckle; "go 'long and tend to your own business. Git your own neck out of the noose 'fore you reach out to help me over a fence. G'-by, Jim."

When Jim got to the mill he found Grierson ready with his weekly report. The old bookkeeper had put in a happy Sunday preparing it. From morning till night he had scratched and crackled in figures and computations—a regular debauch.

"She's coming. She's coming now," Grierson said, his face wrinkling dryly as if the skin were ledger paper. "Shows sixty-five boxes to the machine."

"But shipments are less than ever," Jim said as he glanced over the sheet.

"Cars," said Grierson, shortly. "Goods are in the warehouse, but the railroad won't set in cars to ship them out."

Moran's railroad would not set in cars. This was not altogether unexpected. The railroad could hamper him, delay him—and escape under the plea of a car shortage. Crops were moving. The excuse would hold good. Jim knew he was powerless against this new aggression.

Then came a telegram from New York, driving temporarily from Jim's mind the matter of freight-cars. It was a long telegram:

> German steamer *Dessau* sunk 50,000 boxes pins aboard, bound Bremen to Argentine. Agents Argentine firms offer 70 cents on dock here. Have order 15,000 boxes if can ship ten days. Money on dock. Welliver fill order you cannot.

Seventy cents for pins with the New York market at forty-four cents or thereabouts! A clean killing of nearly fifty-five hundred dollars!

Jim snatched up Grierson's report. It showed seven thousand boxes packed in the warehouse, and estimated twelve thousand boxes unpacked in the bins. He did not wait to weigh consequences or to offset difficulties.

> Accept order. Will ship 15,000 boxes pins ten days this date seventy cents New York.

This message despatched, Jim rushed out into the mill in search of Beam; told him the fact.

"How will we get them packed out?" he asked.

"If you was to ask me serious," said Beam, with a frown, "I'd say you couldn't."

"We've got to. How many are we packing out a day?"

"Close to a thousand boxes. These packers are the limit. They can't get up speed."

"We've got to make some regular shipments. That means about fifteen thousand boxes to pack out in ten days. Put on a double force of packers."

"Where'll I git 'em? We're short now, and no place to go for more."

"Get boys, then," said Jim. "And tell the men—any of them that are willing to work evenings—to come in and pack. We'll run that packing-room twenty-four hours a day if we have to."

"You're the boss," said Beam, dubiously.

Jim went in person to the freight department of the railroad. He made requisition for eight extra cars to be set in within ten days.

"Can't be done," said the freight-agent. "We haven't and won't have the cars."

"You mean you have orders not to set in cars for us, don't you? Well, Mister Freight-Agent, I'm going to have those cars. You see to it they're set in or things'll happen round here."

"You can't bulldoze me," said the man. "I know what I'm doin'. You'll get what cars I set in, and no more. And if you talk too much maybe you won't get any."

Jim glared at the man, half of a mind to haul him over the desk and argue with him physically, but thought better of it and slammed out of the office.

He had to have those cars. It was equally clear the road would not give them to him. What then?

To reach the office again Jim had to pass through the yard where dry lumber for turned stock was piled. There was, he noticed, a reasonable supply, but no heavy stock. More would have to be bought within the month, for his own sawmill had not yet been able to cut out for drying sufficient quantities to carry on operations. Drying, air-drying, requires time. Until his own boards could dry, lumber must be purchased. Thence came the idea.

He hurried to the office and sent wires to Muskegon, to Traverse City, to Reed City, to the big lumber-mills of the section.

> How much two-inch stock can you ship at once. Must come box-cars. Price.

In two hours he had replies, irritated, humorous, bewildered.

"Box-cars? Are you crazy?" one said. Jim grinned. He knew it must sound like lunacy to be ordering lumber of the class he wanted in box-cars. He replied to all, reiterating his demands.

"Fifty cents extra per thousand for loading," came back replies.

"How many cars?" Jim countered. "When?"

Muskegon could ship two cars next day and one the day after. Traverse could ship three cars within three days. Reed City could ship four, on four successive days.

"O. K.," wired Jim. "Let them come hustling."

He had solved his car problem. Moran's road could not stop cars shipped through. They would be set in on Jim's siding and unloaded, and because Jim had requisitions in for cars as yet unsupplied, he could reload them and ship them out again filled with his product.

He called in Grierson.

"I've accepted an order for fifteen thousand pins for Argentine Republic. Price seventy cents New York. To be shipped in ten days."

Grierson threw up his hands. "We haven't the pins. We can't get the cars to ship them."

"We've got the pins, and the cars are on their way to us. Send your young man out after Beam."

The superintendent came in presently.

"I've got ten box-cars of two-inch maple and birch coming in within the next three or four days. Have a gang ready to take care of it. Put on enough extra men in the shipping department to load as fast as the cars empty," he said.

Beam gaped at Jim. Then his eyes brightened, he grinned, he threw back his head and roared.

"Mr. Ashe," he said, when he could speak, "you're a regular feller, and sudden!"

The cars arrived. On the eighth day fifteen thousand boxes of pins were on their way to New York in eight box-cars, and the freight-agent of Moran's railroad looked at Jim with the light of admiration in his eyes. Jim had met a sudden emergency suddenly and efficiently. He was tempted to sit down and describe the feat to his father, who would have delighted in it. But he did not. He remembered Clothespin Jimmy's admonition not to bother him with his business.

But Clothespin Jimmy learned of the matter, which Jim did not know. He learned of it promptly, as he learned most of the details of what went on in the mill, from a source Jim was far from suspecting.

The day after the last car was on its way Zaanan Frame stopped Jim on the street.

"Hain't forgot that strip of timber of old Le Bar's?" he asked.

"No," said Jim.

"Nice afternoon for a drive," said Zaanan, "out toward Le Bar's."

"Very," said Jim, smiling at the old man's manner of handling a situation. "Would you like to go with me?"

"No," said Zaanan, gruffly, "but if I was drivin' that way and come to Bullet's Corners and there wa'n't nobody there, I calc'late I'd slack down and wait till somebody come. G'-by, Jim."

After dinner Jim drove out toward Le Bar's. At Bullet's Corners, waiting in the shade of a big hickory, were Zaanan Frame and his horse Tiffany.

"Howdy," said Zaanan. "Goin' somewheres?"

"Thought I'd call on old man Le Bar," said Jim, playing the game according to Zaanan's rules.

"Goin' that way myself," said Zaanan, with surprise that seemed real. "Calc'late I'll git there 'bout a quarter of an hour first, seem's I've got the best horse."

"You have a fine animal," said Jim, without a quiver.

Zaanan looked over at him suspiciously; gazed at Tiffany's ancient and knobby frame; opened his mouth as though to make an observation, but decided on silence.

"G'-by, Jim," he said, in a moment.

"G'-by, Judge," said Jim.

In an honest fifteen minutes Jim drove on until he saw two old men sitting on the door-step of a house at the roadside. It was a little, weather-beaten house, not such as one would expect to find the owner of a fortune in timber housed in. But one of the men was Zaanan Frame, so Jim stopped and alighted.

"Jim," said Zaanan, "meet Mr. Le Bar. This here's Mr. Ashe, Louis."

"She's yo'ng man," said Louis, with a twinkle.

"Mr. Le Bar figgers he's gittin' on in life," said Zaanan. "He sort of wants to git his affairs settled up on account of maybe bein' called away sudden—"

"When le bon Dieu say," Louis interjected, softly.

"He owns quite a piece of timber," said Zaanan, "and figgered you might have some use for it. Hardwood."

"Yes," said Jim, not knowing what was expected of him. "How many acres?"

"Twenty t'ousand-odd acre," said Louis.

"It'll run twenty to twenty-five thousand beech, birch, and maple to the acre," said Zaanan.

"Diversity Hardwood Company dey hoffer me twelf dollar an acre," said Louis. "But me, I not sell to heem for twenty. I sell not at all till comes dat time w'en I'm ready. Now dat time she's come."

"How much are you asking?"

"First price—twelf dollar and a half; last price—twelf dollar and a half. No dicker."

Jim looked at Zaanan, who nodded.

"I'll take a sixty-day option at that price, if you're agreeable."

"How much for dat option?"

"A thousand dollars," said Jim.

"Ver' good. We make trade, eh? Now Zaanan she write for us a paper."

Zaanan completed the legal details; they smoked and ate of Louis's honey and doughnuts, and started on the return to Diversity.

"Two hundred and fifty thousand dollars," Jim said to Zaanan as their buggies came abreast on a broad stretch of road. "It's a lot of money."

"Um! I've knowed fellers to do a lot with an option down to Grand Rapids."

"What ought I to get for this land?"

"Some folks might go as high as thirteen dollars. But if they was apt to lose it I shouldn't be s'prised if this Diversity Hardwood Company was to go fifteen. It's wuth it to them—or anybody else. But I calc'late I'd git a bonyfidy offer from some other feller 'fore I went to Moran's crowd."

"I calculate so, too," said Jim. Then after a pause: "Why didn't you go into this yourself, Judge? You could have handled it."

"Young feller, I'm past seventy. I got enough so's nobody kin starve me. I hain't chick nor child nor relative on earth. What d'you calc'late I'd do with more 'n I've got? It's come too late for me, Jim. I've sort of give up my aims and ambitions for Diversity, and hain't got none left. Diversity's used me up, sich as I be, and it's welcome to what it got. And me, I guess I got my pay all right. I've seen marryin's and christenin's. I've seen young folks happy and old folks comforted. I've stuck my finger into folkses' pies, and seen 'em with tears in their eyes that was better 'n thanks. No, son, I've had my investment and my profits. You're welcome to yourn."

CHAPTER XVII

It was the following Friday that Jim's attention was called to the scant stock of logs on the skids. He knew that the mill had been eating up more timber than before, and of course was pleased, for that meant an increased production. He knew, too, that the Diversity Hardwood Company had missed sending down a train of logs once or twice when they should have been sent; but other matters had filled his attention to the exclusion of this.

John Beam saw Jim staring at the logs and stepped over to his side.

"I was comin' up to see you about this to-day," he said. "Them folks is givin' us the worst of it, plenty. Look at the logs they're sendin' down. Mostly beech, and dozy at that. For a week we've been short of maple for veneer. And they've been holdin' back on us. We're usin' twice what they're sendin' down. I asked the boss of their train crew what was the matter, and he just grinned at me so's I wanted to land him one, and says we was lucky to be alive."

"Do you think they're trying to tie us up?"

"I don't *think* it," said John.

Jim turned on his heel and strode back to the office. He called the Diversity Company on the telephone.

"We're running short of logs," he said. "You've been cutting down on shipments. When can we have another train-load?"

"Things aren't going just right in the woods," said a voice. "I don't believe we can get you more than a small train-load before Tuesday or Wednesday."

"We'll be shut down Saturday if we don't get logs."

"I'm sorry, Mr. Ashe, but we're doing our best."

"Is Mr. Moran there?"

"He'll be in on the afternoon train."

Jim hung up the receiver. He had been feeling too fine; he had grown cocky at his recent successes; now he had a taste of the opposite emotion. His mill was running better—but what good did it do if the log supply failed? He had been able to borrow money to pay bills and to operate—but that only made matters worse if he were unable to get out his product. He had an option on Le Bar's timber. This might or might not be a profitable matter, but it was of no present help. He must have logs.

That afternoon he was at the depot as the train pulled in. Moran alighted and Jim fastened upon him instantly. "Mr. Moran," he said, "your men are not getting logs to us."

"Um! What seems to be wrong?" Moran's voice was irritating. Jim fancied it was deliberately irritating.

"I'm not here to tell you what's wrong. That's your lookout," Jim said. "Your business is to supply us with logs according to our contract—and if anything interferes it's your job to see it doesn't interfere."

Moran's eyes glinted.

"You'll get logs as we're able to ship them. Our first business is to supply our own mill. You're a side issue."

"That's your attitude, is it? The obligation of contract means very little to you."

"That contract was none of my making, Ashe. And if you don't like the way we carry it out, you have your redress. Go to the courts."

"I guess I've smoked out the reason we aren't getting what we're entitled to," said Jim, his voice rising with his anger. "Its name is Moran—a pretty unsavory reason, from all I gather."

Moran glared.

"You can't talk to me like that, young man. You can't bulldoze me." He started to move away. Jim reached out swiftly, caught the man by the shoulder, and slammed him against the side of the depot.

"I'm not through talking with you," he said, evenly, his eyes beginning to glow. "When I want to talk to a man I don't consider it good manners for him to walk off. Now, Mister Man, you stay put till I've mentioned a few things to you. If you budge I'll fetch you back again."

Moran struggled, cursed, and struck at Jim.

"I don't want to thrash you, Moran," said Jim, "but I can—and I may have to. It depends on you. Stand still!"

Moran turned his savage eyes on the young man's face. What he saw made him hesitate. He ceased to struggle; stood glaring venomously.

"Now listen," said Jim, unconscious of the knot of Diversity's citizens who had gathered about. "You've been needing to hear a few facts and opinions, and to-day's the date of delivery. You and your railroad have been a blight on this county. You're trying to turn the Diversity Company into another blight. So far as I can learn you haven't a decent hair on your head. You're never guilty of a fair and decent act if hard work will show you a crooked way out of it. You've gouged citizens and shippers with your railroad; you've robbed your laborers in the woods. If you have any associates I expect you've cheated them.

"Now you're trying to grab all Diversity and run it as you run your business. You're trying to steal a well-governed, honest town, and turn it into the sort of thing you admire. You came to me and asked me to help you. You want to make this county a little principality, with you as the autocrat. It would be a sad day for Diversity. If the people of this town have the sense the Almighty gave doodle-bugs they'll see what you're up to. You want the courts. You want the machinery of the law, so you can sack the place. Not a man here, not a man in your woods, would be safe in life or property. You could wrong without fear of redress. So far you've been able to get away with it, but I'm thinking the folks here will wake up in time. If you've been a crook with men you've been a miserable brute with women."

Moran cursed again, but Jim quelled his struggle promptly.

"It's astonishing," he went on, "that some woman's brother or father hasn't seen to it you got what you deserve. Some day one of them will."

Jim was surprised into a moment's silence by the sudden grayness that shaded Moran's face, by the expression of furtiveness, of fear, that crept into his eyes.

"Oh, you're a bit afraid of that, eh? You ought to be. Now for personal matters. You think the Ashe Clothespin Company would be a fine property to add to your holdings, so you mixed up with Welliver and his gang to break me. You hired the Kowterskis to spike my logs and to tamper with my machinery, and you saw what happened to one Kowterski. You've tried to hold back cars so I couldn't ship; now you're planning to cut me off on timber. Well, you aren't going to do it." He thought of Marie Ducharme. "And there's another matter, which we won't discuss publicly. If you think hard perhaps you'll guess. That's what made me despise you first. I don't suppose it matters to you how many decent folks despise you, Moran, but it gives me some satisfaction to tell you there are a lot of them. I guess that's about all, except that I've got to have logs—and I'm going to have them." He loosened his hold. Moran moved his head in his released collar, drew a long breath.

"Through, are you? Well, Ashe, see if you're man enough to listen to me without using the strong arm. You've made your talk. Maybe you think you can talk that way to Michael Moran and get away with it. I've a few things to settle with you, and this isn't the least." His partially restrained passion burst its bonds in fury. "I'll get you!" he shouted. "I'll bust you if it takes every dollar I own. Logs! See how many logs you get. Where'll you be by the time the courts give you damages—and by that time the courts will belong to me. You've started in to crowd me, too, you infernal fool. What good do you think that Le Bar option is going to do you? Do you think I'll buy from you? Don't you suppose I can stop a sale to anybody else? You just lose your thousand, that's all. And that last thing that you didn't describe. I know what it is, Ashe, and take a warning from me. Change your boarding-house and get out of my way." He turned, pushed his way violently through the little crowd, and almost ran down the street.

As Jim followed more slowly he heard a man say: "Gosh! I wouldn't be him for consid'able. Wait till Moran gits at him."

Jim rather longed for that moment. He went at once to Grierson's desk.

"Where's our log contract?" he asked. Grierson got it from the safe. Jim jerked it open, read it quickly. His eyes lighted, his teeth clicked. "Listen to this," he said. "Does it mean what it says—legally? 'If for any reason the said Diversity Hardwood Company shall fail to deliver to the said Ashe Clothespin Company logs according to the terms of this contract in sufficient number to fill the requirements of the said Ashe Clothespin Company, then the said Clothespin Company shall have the right to go upon the lands of the Hardwood Company at the most convenient place to them, and to cut timber, take logs from skidways, make use of all tools and appliances belonging to the Hardwood Company which shall be necessary to such logging operations, and this shall include the use of camps, railroads, teams, tools, and any equipment which is available. The cost of such operations shall be faithfully noted and shall be deducted from the contract price of the timber taken in such manner.'"

Grierson peered at Jim through his glasses. "It's a usual clause in such contracts," he said, "and I guess it's legal. But that's as strong a clause as I ever saw. I don't know as I ever heard of one that was enforced."

"This one is going to be," said Jim, shortly. "Go out to the log-yard," he said to Grierson's assistant, "and send Tim Bennett here."

"Tim," said Jim, when the cant-dog man appeared, "there was a time when lumberjacks would fight for their boss."

"Who says I won't?" Tim demanded, belligerently.

"Just wanted to find out," said Jim, with a smile that Tim answered broadly. "Know where there are any more like you?"

"Lumberjacks—real ones—is leavin' this county as fast as they kin go. But there's some left. Shouldn't be s'prised if I could dig up a couple of dozen."

"I want clean men—no boozers—on duty. I want men to depend on in a pinch, who will keep their mouths shut. And I'd just as soon they wouldn't be friends of Michael Moran."

"Mike Moran, is it?" Tim asked, his eyes gleaming. "Are you goin' after him? 'Tis a glad day for Tim Bennett. Friends of Mike's—there hain't no sich animal, Mr. Ashe."

"Find all you can. Don't tell 'em what's up—because you don't know," Jim said, with a twinkle. "Don't get 'em together in a gang, but have 'em meet to-morrow night in that bunch of cedar this side the red bridge. If they happen to have peavey handles they might bring them along."

"To use for canes where the walkin's bad," grinned Tim. "I'll have them there."

Jim was not satisfied. He wired a friend in the old home town:

> Go down Patsy's have him send twenty good boys. Ten on afternoon, ten on morning train to-morrow. With peavey handles.

He knew this would be enough; that Patsy Garrity would send him the men he needed.

Jim wanted advice, but hesitated to ask it. He knew Zaanan Frame was his friend, but the old man was on the side of law and order. He might frown on Jim's intention, for, lawful as it was, it might, probably would, turn out to be anything but orderly or peaceful. Still, he decided to go.

Zaanan listened to him quietly, let him finish without comment.

"Blood's young," he said at the end, and wagged his head. "But this time I calc'late there hain't no other way. Moran hain't got no use for law, but he'll go rushin' off for a temp'rary injunction. That'll tie you up till he kin collect his army. If I was doin' this I calc'late I'd git there first. Eh? See young Bob Allen that's runnin' for prosecutor. He'll draw the bill for you. You're startin' in on a real job, Jim. Better be reasonable sure you're ready to finish it 'fore you start in. G'-by, Jim."

Jim went to Bob Allen. The young lawyer's eyes shone as he listened.

"It's coming to him," he said. "Moran's been needing somebody to handle him without tongs. Mr. Ashe, if I get to be prosecutor, and you'll back me,

I'll chase him round in circles. I'll do it whether you back me or not. We want to handle this right. When do you plan to land your invasion?"

"About midnight to-morrow."

"Then Judge Scudder's due to have his rest broken. I'll be at his house at midnight with the papers—and a deputy. He'll issue the injunction, all right. By that time you'll be in full blossom. The deputy will slide off to serve the restraining order. Gosh! I'd like to be along with you."

"I'd like to have you," said Jim, heartily. "We've never had time to get acquainted, but I guess we're going to. Eh?"

"You bet you!" said Allen. "This place has been drifting along to the graveyard. It's a godsend to have somebody come along that's sudden. From what I hear you're sudden enough to suit anybody—judging from your little love-feast with Moran this afternoon."

"I suppose the citizens are holding a funeral over me."

"Yes. But they're thinking, too. You mentioned a few things that gave them something to think about. I don't figure you did Peleg Goodwin's campaign a heap of good. It's going to be a fight, though. Moran's spending money."

"The next prosecutor ought to have legal evidence of it," said Jim.

"By Jove!" Allen exclaimed, "that's something I overlooked. If evidence is to be had I'll get it."

Jim went back to the office to study a map of the section and to lay the plans for his campaign.

CHAPTER XVIII

That night Tim Bennett's lumberjacks began to drift in. There were Danes, Frenchmen, Irish, a sprinkling of Indians. They did not linger in Diversity, nor did they congregate, but passed quickly through with a cheerful air. There was exhilaration, anticipation, in their eyes, whether of Scandinavian blue or of aboriginal black. Old times were back again. For a moment a decadent age of which they despaired was returning to better manners, and there was to be a fight. Peavey handles! There was joy to be had from the very sound of it. In the morning a scattering of big men, predominantly Irish, got off the train and straggled away. In the afternoon another group arrived. They came so quietly, so unostentatiously, that Diversity was hardly aware of them. A full fifty were on hand—fifty fighting-men such as no other set of conditions has produced, men who fought and worked for the joy of it. A race of men who worked, not for pay, but because they loved the work, is worthy of chronicle. They live no more. Men whose highest wage was the knowledge that their camp or crew, or they individually, had done more and harder and better work than some other camp or crew or individual have resident in them something that should be handed down through time for other generations to admire. They possessed vices, but they were brief, flaming, roaring safety-valve vices, almost epic in themselves. For months they were accustomed to live austere, laborious, loyal lives in the ramps. Then for a day, a week, they appeared among their fellows, and their fellows received them and robbed them and plied them with liquor and directed their splendid energies into ways of debauchery. On the scales of justice the robust virtue of them outweighs their brief, primitive descents into the depths. They were men.

Tim Bennett reported to Jim Ashe. "They're here, fair bustin' with the thought of it. The taste of a fight is in their mouths and they're rollin' it under their tongues."

"Good men?"

"Mr. Ashe," said Tim, joyously, "I'd undertake to drive logs through hell with 'em—and the devil throwin' rocks from the shore."

"Any talk in town?"

"Not a peep. Them boys sneaked through like the shadow of a flock of hummin'-birds. They're keepin' quiet where they are without even a bit of a song. By night there'll be so much deviltry penned up in 'ere lookin' for a place to bust out, that when it does come Moran'll think a herd of boilers is blowin' up round him."

"Go out, then, and keep them quiet. I'll be along by ten to-night."

It was not Jim's intention to descend upon the Diversity Hardwood Company with his men blindly and to seize what might by good fortune fall into his hands. He had planned well, as a good general plans. Simultaneously he would strike at several points, so that in a single moment, if all went well, the machinery he needed to move logs would be in his hands. He was ready.

Satisfied he had done all he could do to make success certain, Jim went home to the widow's to supper. He was excited. Appetite was lacking. He felt inside very much like a countryman descending for the first time in a swift elevator. It was not fear; it was not excitement; it was all the nerves of his body setting and bracing themselves, making ready to respond to strain.

He scarcely touched his food; sat silently reviewing his plans to make sure every point was checked up, that there would be no omissions, no mistake. The widow watched him out of the corner of her shrewd eye; Marie Ducharme watched him, too, less shrewdly, with a different sort of glance. Marie's eyes were dark with much brooding; were circled by drab shadows drawn by the finger of mental anguish. If Jim had looked at her he would have seen again that hungry look with which she followed the departing train—but now it was bent upon himself.

The widow withdrew to the kitchen, not obviously, but with sufficient pretext. She sensed a quarrel; she saw in Jim's silence and lack of appetite an ailment of the heart, not a business worry. She fancied Marie's face spoke of willingness to be reconciled—and eliminated herself to give the difficulty a chance to right itself. Widows have a way of seeing more love-affairs than are visible to other eyes—more, in fact, than are in being.

Presently Marie spoke:

"Jim," she said. It was the first time she had called him by his first name. "Jim, I want to go somewhere, do something, to-night. I want to get away from this house."

Jim looked at her a moment, and she was hurt to see he was not thinking of her, had hardly understood her words. Perhaps she, too, had put on his silence the same interpretation as the widow.

"Go somewhere?" he said, vaguely, then flushed at his awkwardness. "I'm sorry, Marie. I was a long way off when you spoke. It was rude, wasn't it? But I've had such a heap of things to think about these last days that some of them insist on hanging round outside of business hours. Has something happened? Any trouble with Mrs. Stickney?"

"No. No trouble. I just want to get away. I want you to talk to me and keep me from thinking about myself—and some things. I—I'm afraid tonight, Jim."

Jim bit his lip boyishly.

"Confound it!" he said. "I simply can't get away to-night. Business. But don't I wish I could go with you some place—and talk to you. There are things I wanted to say to you the other night, Marie, that—well, I guess it took time for me to think of. I want to talk to you about the same thing, for I've been thinking about the same thing. I was too abrupt. You were right to give me the answer you did—but I've got some more arguments now, a lot of them."

Marie's face softened. How boyish, how eagerly boyish he was!

"You mustn't talk about that," she said, gently. "I can't change. Your work is here. You're tied to it. And I must get away from it—to stay. Can't you understand? Don't misunderstand me, Jim. It wasn't to give you a chance to ask me to reconsider that I asked you to go out with me. No. No. It was to have you to talk to. To have the consciousness that I was with a man—a man who—was—a human being." Her voice faltered. "I wanted you to say to me some of the things you have said before—about people being good, about the world being good, about faith and trustworthiness and honor. I don't know those things, but I want to hear about them—to-night. Because I'm afraid."

"Afraid of what?"

"Afraid of—myself. I talked to you that first day we met—more than I should. So you know me. I am the same girl I was then, but I am not the same girl. Then I knew it would be possible for me to choose the—bitter way. To choose it deliberately as a way of escape. But I did not know then how bitter that way would be. Now I know I should not choose it deliberately, but be forced into it by—by myself."

"You mustn't talk that way, I won't have you say that sort of thing about—my girl."

"It's true, and I am afraid. Can't your business step aside for to-night?"

"It can't, Marie. If it were an ordinary night or an ordinary matter that calls me, I would stay." He stopped, considered. It was his nature to speak little of his affairs, to offer few confidences. To tell Marie the truth seemed his only honorable way of escape from the dilemma. "I'll tell you about it," he said, with sudden decision, "and you will understand."

Then he told her, from the beginning in his father's library. He described his difficulties, his war with the Clothespin Club, his bitterer war with Michael Moran. He told her what Moran had done and was seeking to do. He told her his measures of defense and of counter-attack, and particularly the plan for to-night. "And so you see," he ended, "I must go."

"Yes," she said, slowly, "you must go. And Michael Moran has done those things? You must hate him!"

"Yes," said Jim, "but not for what he has done to me. I hate him because—" He hesitated, unable to bring himself to utter the thought in connection with Marie.

"Because?" Marie questioned.

"Because," said Jim, between his teeth, "he is planning and working to make you take the choice you have talked about without appreciating what you were saying."

"Yes," said Marie, her eyes shut as though to hide from her a painful sight—"yes, he is doing that. And I have known what I was saying, Jim. I know what I am saying now. I wish you could have stayed with me to-night, Jim. I'm afraid—afraid." She arose and ran from the room.

When Jim left the house it was with a troubled mind. He did not understand Marie; she was not fathomable by him. The evening's zest of adventure lay cold within him.

Shortly after eight o'clock he drove away from the livery barn. As he drove past the Widow Stickney's street he glanced toward the house and saw Michael Moran entering the yard. What he did not see was Marie Ducharme leaving by the back way, hurrying as though pursued, making her way to the edge of town and beyond—beyond until she arrived at the hummock where she and Jim had first spoken. And there she crouched, looking off to the southwest where a silver gleam of the great lake was visible between the trees. It grew darker, but she did not move; dew fell upon her shoulders, chilling her; the lake breeze penetrated her thin garments, but she replied only with a shiver. Her hands were clenched on her breast. "Help me! Help me!" she whispered her soul crying to a Power outside herself.

CHAPTER XIX

The moon lighted Jim Ashe to the spot where Tim Bennett and his company of lumberjacks waited. It must be confessed that Jim's thoughts on the way had more to do with Marie Ducharme than with the enterprise of the night. He thought of Michael Moran, too; hoped in a vague sort of way that the night might bring him face to face with Moran in not peaceful circumstances, for he was young enough to feel the need of settling scores in a physical manner.

Bennett and the men were awaiting him impatiently, though he arrived a full half-hour before his time. They crowded about him, appraising him as a leader, for many of them had never seen him before. He satisfied them. Bennett had told them stories of Sudden Jim which they approved. The result was that they were willing, eager to follow wherever he might lead, careless of consequences to themselves.

"I worked for your dad," shouted a huge Irishman. "Then you worked for a better man than I," said Jim.

"It's a proper son that admits the same," replied the man.

"Boys," said Jim, "we may have a tough job this night and we may have an easy one. We'll figure it at its toughest. You came without knowing why you were coming. I'll tell you. We're going to seize the Diversity Hardwood Company's logging railroad; we're going to take charge of the rolling stock. We're going to capture Camp One with all the logs we can get, and enough standing timber to cut what we need. There's a fair gang in Camp One, but mostly Poles and Hunkies and Italians."

"L'ave us at 'em!" bellowed the big Irishman. "Shut up and listen," said Jim, sharply; and the Irishman grinned delightedly. That was the way to speak up to a man.

"The engine is in the roundhouse. Ten trucks stand on the siding near it. There are twenty more trucks at the landings by Camp One. Can anybody here run a locomotive?"

"Me," said a stocky Dane.

"There'll be nobody there but a watchman or so. Take ten men and make for town. Land on that roundhouse at eleven o'clock. Hitch on to the trucks and scoot for the woods with them. Pick your own men and start now. The rest of us hike across lots to Camp One. You didn't forget peavey handles, I see." Jim grinned down at them and leaped from his buggy.

The parties separated, one moving townward, the other into the woods in the direction of the Diversity Company's cuttings. With the latter went Jim.

They marched through the moonlit woods gaily as to a merrymaking, but withal as silently as such men could march. They jostled one another, slyly tripped one another, found delight in holding down springy saplings so they would spring back to switch the ears of the man coming behind. It was a picnic of big boys—which would be no picnic when they stripped and got down to business.

For half an hour they stumbled along. An unexpected voice called from the obscurity ahead.

"Mr. Ashe."

"What is it?" Jim demanded. He knew here was none of his own men; wondered who else was abroad in the woods at that time of night. "Who is it?"

"Gilders," said the man, stepping into view. The rifle, which seemed as much a part of his usual costume as his floppy hat, was under his arm. He stopped, was surrounded by Jim's lumberjacks.

"What are you doing here at this time of night?" Jim demanded.

"I am here—many places—at what time of night is best," said Gilders. "Night or day—what's the difference?" He shrugged his shoulders. "I cut across from town to catch you. Moran's warned. He's got a dozen men at the roundhouse. They've telephoned the camps."

Moran warned! It seemed impossible. Who could have given warning? Jim named over mentally those who knew what was afoot. Zaanan Frame—he had not talked. Allen—he, too, was a safe man. Grierson—oxen could not have drawn a word from him. Marie Ducharme? She knew. Jim had seen Moran going to her but an hour before. Marie Ducharme. He would not believe she could be guilty of such a betrayal of confidence. It was not in her to commit such an act. Yet she had not seemed herself. Something had happened. She had been afraid. Jim closed his eyes, bit his under lip. No one else who knew could have given the warning. The opportunity had been hers. The logic of events bore against her.

Jim turned to Gilders.

"Can you lead me to town the way you came?"

"Yes."

"Tim Bennett, you're boss of the gang that goes to the camp. I'll take ten men away from you. You'll have thirty—it ought to be enough. You"—he pointed to a man—"come with me, and you and you and you." He selected his men. "On the jump," he said to Gilders, and at the heels of their guide they plunged headlong to re-enforce the party that had gone before.

Jim held a match to his watch. It was fifteen minutes past ten. They had three-quarters of an hour to reach a point that could not be reached in less than an hour. When they arrived the battle for the roundhouse would have been on a quarter of an hour. If Moran's party were strong enough that quarter of an hour might spell defeat for the whole enterprise. If the first attacking party could hold out until Jim arrived—

"Hustle," Jim said, briefly, and saved his breath for the exertion before him.

The men went silently now, grimly. The smell of imminent battle was in their noses. Ahead of them were comrades facing uneven odds. It was not simply to fight that they hurried, but to succor their friends. Jim's legs, untrained to woods travel, cried out for rest, but his will compelled them on.

At last lights shone below them, the black tube of the Diversity Company's smokestack lifted into the star-shimmering sky—ten minutes would take them to it. They heard a sudden, distant shout, other shouts, a babel of sounds subdued by distance. The fight for the roundhouse was on. The attacking party had struck, had met surprising resistance.

"Run!" shouted Jim.

They ran, stumbling, falling headlong. Men's breath came pantingly; bruised shins were paid for in brief oaths. Each man sought to outdistance his fellows, to be first to add his weight to the tide of battle.

Down the last gully they charged, across the flat before the mills, over the tracks. Before them loomed the roundhouse, now bright with electric light. Before the big doors swayed and writhed a group of men. Other dark figures, two and two, quaintly intertwined, moved and struggled and smote like living silhouettes. Hoarse shouts arose; the thud of blows; the shuffling of feet came to Jim's ears. Then he was in the midst of it.

Even with the addition of Jim's reinforcements his party was outnumbered; but Moran's men, under the shock and surprise of the charge, gave way, but only for an instant. Inside, Jim saw the engine, steam up, a man in the cab. They were getting ready to bring it out. Why? he asked himself, even as the sight of it was shut out and he was hemmed in by fighting men.

It was Jim's first real fight. It came to him suddenly that he could fight, that he was worthy to stand side by side with these lumberjacks, to give blows where they gave blows, and he was glad.

Again he caught a brief glimpse of the interior of the roundhouse as a man before him went down under a blow from his fist. On the tender he saw Michael Moran—not fighting, but watching, directing. He saw a man break away from the melee and leap toward the engine, recognized Gilders. His teeth were bared, his hands empty. Jim struggled forward, shot another look, saw Moran, his face distorted with rage, raise a chunk of coal above his head and hurl it. Whether it found its mark or not Jim could not tell.

Jim's men were holding their own. Though outnumbered, they were trained to battle of this sort, with inherited talent for it, against men not bred to fight with their hands. But Moran's men fought, and fought well. Numbers made them even, if not superior.

It was apparent they had been told to guard the big door, for as best they could they remained solidly before it. They were not men to take the offensive on their own initiative, nor, Jim thought, would they assume it under orders unless the enemy were in actual retreat. It was a point to be taken advantage of. He wormed and wriggled out of the fight, marked the Dane who could drive an engine, and hauled him out, struggling. At random the two of them separated two others from the confusion.

"The engine," Jim panted. "Side door. Come on!"

They scurried to a small door left unguarded, and plunged through. The engine was before them, Moran still on the tender. On the ground lay Gilders. Moran's missile had flown true. The Dane with his companions stormed the cab. In an instant they had hurled down the engineer, hurled him so ungently that he did not rise. Jim dodged a lump of coal which Moran hurled, and himself threw a peavey handle which he had picked up somewhere in the fight. It caught Moran amidships so that he crumpled up on the coal, the breath knocked from his overnourished, undertrained body. Jim scrambled to his side, lifted him and dumped him off with scant regard for how or where he fell.

"Toot the whistle!" he yelled. "Back her out."

The whistle screeched, and in that confined space its voice was the voice of many demons. The wheels began to turn.

"One man up here," Jim ordered, and when the man came he set an example by lifting his voice in battle-cry, by hurling lumps of coal at the backs of the defenders.

They turned. Taken in the rear by a new enemy, menaced by a down-bearing locomotive, their morale departed, they scattered to each side, broke, some even turned in sudden flight. Jim's lumberjacks did the rest.

The locomotive moved out on a clear track, backed to the switch where stood the empty trucks. It was Jim who coupled them to the engine.

"We've done the job here," he said to the big Irishman who was his companion on the tender. "Collect the boys and load 'em on the trucks. We're off for the woods. Maybe Bennett's gang is chewing on more than it can swallow. Somebody see to Gilders inside there."

A few moments more saw the little army perched precariously on the trucks. They were bruised, bleeding, clothing was in tatters, eyes were draped in black, clearings appeared where once had grown strong white teeth. But they were jubilant, for victory had been theirs. They celebrated it noisily.

Slowly, with great rattling and jangling, with song and cheer, they moved away from the roundhouse, out of the yard and out upon the narrow-gauge track which led back into the woods. Five miles of uncomfortable travel lay between them and Camp One, but its discomforts were not detectable by them. They had won. It had been a fight worth while, and they had won. Another fight lay before them perhaps. They hoped so.

Perhaps Jim Ashe did not know it, but he had tied these men to him with bonds of admiration. From this day they were his friends, would work for him, fight for him. He had fought shoulder to shoulder with them. His quick thought had turned the day in their favor. He was a man who dared, a man who stood on his two feet and wielded fist or peavey handle like a man—he was one of them.

"What's the matter with Sudden Jim?" somebody yelled.

"He's all right," answered back a tumultuous shout, and Jim was more than pleased. He had been tendered an honor which he knew how to appreciate.

"Look out for Crab Creek Trestle," the Irishman said. "If Moran was on the job he'd jerk a rail and treat us to a drop into the marsh."

"Slack down at Crab Creek," Jim shouted to his engineer. He scrambled forward to the cab, and sat looking forward where the headlight peered ahead, illuminating the track.

"She's bane joost ahead," said the engineer. In a moment the trestle came into view. As the light rested on it two black figures emerged from the underbrush to run out upon the structure, where they stopped. The sound of sledge striking steel came back distinctly through the clear air.

Jim leaped from the engine, half a dozen men at his heels. Out upon the trestle they ran, all undesirable risks for an accident insurance company at the minute. The sledge continued to rise and fall, but when Jim was within fifty feet of the men they dropped their implements over the edge and ran. Jim stopped to appraise the damage. His men kept up the pursuit with success, for in a moment he heard a shout of glee and saw a man performing antics in the air as he descended into the marsh muck below.

Moran's men had been too slow. Another minute or so and a rail would have been loosened, but their few blows had not sufficed. The trestle was safe to pass.

"Four men stop here," Jim said, and motioned the train on.

Ten minutes more and they were at Camp One. There were noises of frolic, but none of battle.

"Get cheated out of your fight?" Jim asked Tim Bennett as the cant-dog man hurried up to the engine.

"Not what you could notice," grinned Tim, displaying a split lip and barked knuckles. "But they was Wops or somethin'. We chased 'em into the cook-shanty, where they bide in fear and tremblin'."

"Is there enough moon to load those trucks?"

Tim looked at Jim and grinned broadly.

"There wouldn't be for anybody but you, Mr. Ashe, but these here boys 'u'd work for you if it was so dark you couldn't feel a pin stick into you."

"Leave enough men to hold the gang in the cook-shanty. Take the rest and load. How many trucks can that engine haul down?"

"Twenty, on a pinch."

"Pick as much maple as you can," said Jim. "You're boss."

Given landings, twoscore men who know how to use cant-hooks can handle an astonishing number of logs in an hour. Twenty trucks were not filled in sixty minutes, but the train was ready before dawn—twenty trucks carrying thirty-five thousand feet of hardwood logs.

"Now the cook-shanty," said Jim. "We need it."

The crew rollicked to the log house which was cook-shanty at one end, bunkhouse at the other. Jim parleyed.

"Come out and we'll let you go," he called.

Thoroughly frightened, the foreigners emerged.

"Hit for town," Jim told them. "Your job's gone. Start walking and keep it up—we'll be behind you and it won't be healthy if we catch up."

Half an hour later Jim's crew were breakfasting on Moran's coffee and salt pork. It was a species of humor they could enjoy. The night, with its incidents, had furnished them a story to be told on many evenings in diverse places.

"Fifteen men on the train," Jim ordered. "The rest load the other ten trucks. We'll be back for 'em if Moran doesn't eat us somewhere along the road."

Jim rode back in the engine cab, tired, but filled with a notable satisfaction. He knew he had scored heavily, though his victory was by no means permanent. Altogether, perhaps, he was more pleased with himself than the state of affairs quite warranted. The engineer reminded him of this by asking what they were to do for coal when the supply in the tender was exhausted. Jim could give no reply.

However, he gave his reply after the train of logs had passed the Diversity Company's mills, passed them to an accompaniment of cheers and jeers from the men riding on the trucks. For Jim had seen two cars of coal standing on a siding.

"There's our coal," he said to the engineer. "We'll borrow it on the way back."

And borrow it they did, calmly, under the noses of the enemy.

One more trip to Camp One and return Jim made that day. Another thirty-odd thousand feet of timber was unloaded in his log-yard. He left Tim Bennett in charge, directing him to handle logs as he had never handled them before, and himself went to his office.

Beam and Nelson followed him gleefully. But the surprise of the day was supplied by Grierson, who emerged from his bookkeeping lair, his eyes not free from a moisture the origin of which was open to suspicion, and grasped Jim's hand.

"I wish your father could have been here to see it," he said, and retreated hastily behind his barrier again.

CHAPTER XX

Diversity chattered and gesticulated, surmised and prophesied. It did not know exactly what had happened, but was able to relate much more than had happened. The one protruding fact was that Michael Moran had the worst of the affair. The Ashe Clothespin Company was sawing logs which Moran had intended they should not saw, and young Jim Ashe bounded to local fame—not altogether admirable. The character assigned him was a patchwork of daredevil, Machiavelli, business genius, general, pugilist, bandit, patriot. It depended on whom you talked with which attribute was set foremost.

By night some credit had been subtracted from Jim to be piled up before Zaanan Frame's door as censure. The idea had been circulated subtly. A reign of lawlessness was to be inaugurated. Zaanan Frame, the county's dictator, winked at it, even lent his aid to it. He had debauched the courts themselves, so that, instead of giving their protection to Moran, assailed in his sacred rights of property, they actually issued injunctions forbidding him to interfere with men who, to all intents, were stealing his timber.

Peleg Goodwin made a speech about it from the steps of the hotel, and many good citizens believed him. Jim discovered suddenly he had become an important part of the political issue.

When supper-time came he walked down the road, hesitated in front of the hotel, half of a mind to eat there, for he did not want to meet Marie Ducharme yet. In his office he had been thinking of her, had been trying to argue himself into a belief in her fidelity; but it had been futile. The evidence seemed proof incontrovertible to him. He believed she had betrayed his confidence to Michael Moran.

His hesitation was brief. With a shrug of his shoulders he went on to the widow's. As well have the meeting now as any time, he thought. He was young; he had given his heart, his faith wholly, and his spirit was sick with the shock of disillusionment. Where he loved he had been betrayed— wantonly, it seemed to him. So he went grimly to the widow's table. His face might have borne a far different expression could he have known Marie Ducharme had not closed her eyes through the night, nor till mid-morning brought assurances of his safety. Tenderness and pity might have mingled in his heart could he have known of her struggle on the little hilltop under the moon. But he did not know.

"H'm!" said the widow, as he entered. "Fine carryin's-on! I've had boarders and boarders, but I don't call to mind none been as like to get hauled out from under my roof by the sheriff as you. What you mean by it, anyhow?"

"I don't think the sheriff will interfere with me," said Jim, humorlessly, forgetting or neglecting to greet Marie with even a nod of the head.

"Them that lives by the sword shall die by the sword," the widow said, seeking the support of the Scriptures.

"And those who live by logs must have logs," said Jim.

"Folks is sayin' Zaanan Frame was back of this caper of yours. 'Tain't so, is it?"

"No."

"Knew he wouldn't be lendin' his countenance to murderin' and killin' and maimin' and injurin'."

"There would have been no fighting," said Jim, his eyes on the tablecloth, "if my plans hadn't been betrayed to Moran."

"Who done that, I'd like to know?" said the widow, quick to change her front. "Who'd 'a' done such a miserable, sneakin', low-down thing as that? You ought to ketch him and teach him sich a lesson he wouldn't forgit it in a hurry."

"I can't," said Jim, dully. "You see, it wasn't a man."

"H'm! Serves you right, then, for lettin' a woman find out what you was goin' to do."

Jim made no reply, did not lift his eyes, so he was unconscious of the look Marie bent upon him. Her eyes were startled, dark with apprehension. His manner toward her, what did it mean? Did he suspect her? She bit her lip and pretended to eat. Presently she excused herself and left the room with lagging steps.

Jim finished his meal silently. He, too, went out, his feet heavy as his heart as he descended the steps and walked along the bricked path to the gate. Marie was waiting for him.

"Jim," she said, "what did you mean? You acted so—what you said—"

"I meant," said Jim, dully, "that within an hour from the time I told you what I was going to do, Moran was warned."

"You believe that I warned him?"

He was silent.

"No!" she cried. "No! I didn't see Moran last night, Jim. I didn't see him. I didn't tell him."

"You only make it worse," he said. "Moran was here. I saw him turn in the gate."

"I wasn't here, Jim. I didn't see him. I ran away from him because I was afraid. You don't know how afraid of him I am, Jim. I begged you to stay home last night—but you couldn't; so I ran away. He comes, Jim, and shows me the world—out there. He offers it to me—and I want it, I want it! He doesn't put things into words; but I—I understand him. I—I hate him! But the longing; this awful place—You said you loved me, Jim, and I wouldn't accept your love. You didn't love me, you couldn't love me, or you wouldn't believe—"

"I loved you and I trusted you. I would have trusted you with everything a man can trust a woman with. And you—you hardly waited till I was out of sight before you told him."

She looked at him with agony in her eyes.

"I'll tell you. Yes, I'll tell you, and then you must believe. I—I did love you, Jim, even when I refused you. It is true. You make me tell you. And last night—out there on that knoll—I found I couldn't go on without you. I saw things clearly. I understood what love meant. And my fear of him went away, because I was going to let you know, and then I would be safe—safe with you. Oh, Jim, I was not with him one second. I was out there, sending my heart after you. Now you believe me, don't you, Jim?" Her voice was pitiful.

Each word Jim uttered seemed a bit torn grimly from his heart. He did not believe her. Now that his trust in her was gone, his unbelief grew and multiplied.

"I am a new-comer in your life," he said. "Moran has been there for years. You—he saw you attracted me. That became useful to him. Last night shows how useful. Why do you say these things to me about love? Love is not a thing to lie about. I know what love is, because you—some one I thought was you—had made it live in me. I don't believe you now. I shall never believe you again. The thing you have just said is not true. I believe you have said it—in obedience to him. So he might have an eye which would look into my very soul."

He stopped. She stood silent, pale, her lips parted as in horror. One hand crept upward flutteringly, stopped at her breast, moved outward toward Jim.

"Jim!" she whispered. "Jim! You didn't say that. Tell me I didn't hear that. Tell me! Tell me! You don't know what you're saying, what you're doing. I had won. I had struggled and won. Don't send me back to him." Suddenly she gave way and threw herself on a bench beside the path, her hands over her ears as though to shut out some dreadful sound. "It's a lie!" she panted. "A lie! A lie! A lie!"

Jim felt himself near the breaking-point. He turned and hurried, almost ran, out of the widow's garden, but even as far as the gate he could hear her voice repeating: "A lie! A lie! A lie!"

CHAPTER XXI

All next day train-loads of logs came down from Camp One to be decked in Jim's yard. Thirty-five thousand feet had been rolled off the first night and day; upward of forty thousand feet were added to it the second. It was enough to supply the saws for a week. Moran had made no visible move; no attempt to interfere with the men in the woods or with the running of trains had been made. This did not reassure Jim. Moran was not the man to be beaten so easily. He knew he would strike back—that the Clothespin Club would strike back—for Moran and the Club were as one in this war.

The blow came from the Club—one not altogether unlooked for. It was their logical move, but it would be costly to them. News of it came in telegrams from Jim's agents, telling him that Welliver and Jenkins and Plum were offering clothespins at a further cut of ten per cent. in price.

Jim figured rapidly. He knew that now his mill was running efficiently, his crew of operators were trained, each machine was showing its production of seventy-five boxes of pins or better a day, he was making pins more cheaply than any other manufacturer in the country. He knew they could not make pins at such a price; that every box sold at such a figure represented a loss. It represented a loss to Jim of something like a cent and a half a box. Probably it meant from three to five cents to the Club. But they could stand it for a time. They had capital in reserve. Jim had none, or very little, to carry on an extended war. But fight he had to, whether he had the money or not.

Perhaps he could borrow more, but he very much doubted it. One resource he had—the option on old Louis Le Bar's timber. That must be sold at once.

He determined to take the afternoon train to Grand Rapids to go over it in the big lumber offices. His immediate action was to wire his representatives generally to take no orders at the new price. To New York and Chicago he gave directions to sell one car-load each at a drop of five per cent. under the Club's last figure. This would serve further to demoralize the markets in those centers and to compel the Club to protect its customers on the additional decline. It would cost Jim a few hundreds of dollars. How much more expensive it would be to the Club he did not know.

The morning found him in Grand Rapids. The lumbermen received him with suspicion. It was apparent they were aware of his existence, had expected his arrival. They were willing to talk, but not to deal. They knew the Le Bar tract, of course. It was desirable, but none of them cared to undertake it.

Their attitude was difficult to understand until one old gentleman bruskly informed Jim he did not care to spend his good money buying a lawsuit.

"Why a lawsuit?" Jim asked.

"We were tipped off to you, young man. From a dependable source we know there's something wrong with that tract, and we're taking no chances on it."

"Have you investigated it? Will you investigate it?"

"No. It's a desirable tract, but it's not necessary. We can get along without it, and just now we're too busy to go fooling round with a doubtful title."

"You can easily investigate the title."

"What's the use? We know your option is disputed. We know we'd take on a lawsuit with it, and we don't need any lawsuits."

At last Jim understood. Moran had taken his steps, as he said he would. He had promised that Jim would be unable to dispose of his option, and had made good his promise. The task had been simple. He had notified all possible buyers that he would contest Jim's option; that he claimed some lien on title. Jim knew when he came face to face with the impassable. He put his option in his pocket and returned to Diversity.

Neither magazine nor newspaper could hold his attention on the train. His mind could not be made to forget the weight that lay upon it; his heart could not be numbed to pain by anaesthetic. Jim was young. Suffering was new to him, and experience had not showed him how best to endure it.

It was not the ruin that hung over his business that clouded with anguish the eyes he fixed on the scudding landscape. It was not the knowledge that he was in a corner, fighting for his financial life with his back to the wall. It was Marie—only Marie. Youth can look forward to the building of another fortune; the losses of to-day will be wiped out in the gains of to-morrow. But when love crashes down in sordid ruin there is no to-morrow. Youth cannot see that the unguent of time will close the wound; it can see only that hope, the sweet anticipations which make of the future a magical realm almost within the grasp of the extending hand, has been swept away beyond recall.

Marie was not true, steadfast, as he had believed; her soul did not shine clearly, purely, with the guiding light he thought he had seen. Marie, the wonderful, the womanly, was erased from the picture; replaced by one sordid, despicable, treacherous even. Perhaps the bitterest pain is rending asunder of the trust of youth.

What remained? Work, feverish exertion, the comfort of facing an antagonist, of straining breast to breast with him.

At the junction Jim changed to the Diversity railroad. In the smoker when he entered was a sprinkling of Diversity folk, who, as the train got in motion, edged together to talk politics. Politics in Diversity was a topic of conversation as it had not been for twenty years. Zaanan Frame had taken the zest from it. He had been the county's politics so long. In the eyes of the inhabitants the present condition assumed almost the importance of a revolution.

"Zaanan's beat, and he knows it," was an opinion boldly expressed. "He hain't even makin' a fight for it. Calc'late he's too old."

"Calc'late," replied a gesticulating individual, "he's plum disgusted. Who's the best friend Diversity folks has had, eh? Zaanan Frame; that's who. And now, because a dollar for a vote is easy money to earn, men that ought to think shame is turnin' against him. It hain't that he can't fight. Don't git sich an idee into your head. It's that he's too disgusted to fight."

"He's run things long enough. Nobody kin call his soul his own. He comes perty clost to sayin' who shall marry who, and which kind of a baby they'll have after they're married. We hain't goin' to stand that kind of thing much longer. No, sir; we're a-goin' to run our own affairs like we want to—"

"You're a-goin' to swap Zaanan Frame for Michael Moran, that's what you're goin' to do—and you're welcome to your bargain. Wait till Moran gits the power Zaanan's got now. See how he uses it. Has any feller here got a word to say ag'in Zaanan's honesty? Eh?"

Nobody replied.

"Kin anybody here lay his hand on a wrong Zaanan's done? Kin anybody p'int to a case in court that hain't come out as near fair and just as human men kin make it? No, you can't. But wait. Why d'you calc'late Moran is reachin' out for Zaanan's place? It's so he can chase the law out and put Mike Moran's will in. That's why. It's so he kin make of Diversity what Quartus Hembly made of Owasco a few years back. He'll rob you and git his courts to back him up; there'll be wrongs done and nobody punished. Diversity is run by Zaanan Frame because we've turned over the job to him. But it's run like an American town. Moran'll run it like a town in Roosian Siberier. Mark me!"

"I call to mind the times 'fore Zaanan got his office first," piped up a toothless octogenarian. "Diversity and Hell was first cousins. Sich things as

I've seen! Wa-al, Zaanan he turned to, and 'twa'n't long 'fore there wa'n't a quieter, better-behaved town in the timber. He's deserved a heap of this town."

"He's gone too far. Kind of figgers he's king, or somethin' like that. We hain't goin' to stand for it no more."

"Go ahead," squeaked the old man; "whatever you git is comin' to you. 'Twon't be a year 'fore you're on your knees prayin' for Zaanan Frame to come back, and it'll be too late, 'cause this Moran'll have the power and nobody'll git it away from him."

"Zaanan's beat," repeated the first speaker.

"Looks so," admitted the old man; "but money done it. Votes has been bought, lies has been told. He hain't beat fair."

Jim was interested in spite of himself. Here was a fight, one more fight for him to get into. He, clearer than these men, saw what it would mean to the town and county for Moran to become its dictator. He welcomed another task; it would coax his mind away from Marie. If the new task was also a high duty of citizenship it was so much the more welcome. He sat erect in his seat; again he was Sudden Jim. He addressed the men within hearing.

"Zaanan Frame isn't beaten," he said. "Maybe he won't fight for himself, but there are folks who will fight for him, and I'm one of them. The time's short, but, you men who are against him, take this thought away with you: If you've taken money for your votes or influence, begin to worry. If there has been crookedness you may carry word from me to the man who is to blame for it that he shall answer for his crookedness. The time's short, as I said, but a lot of fighting can be done in a short time. It isn't too late."

"And you're some fighter, Mr. Ashe," grinned a little Irishman. "When you come into the car I says to my friend, says I, 'There's an illigant lad wid knuckles to his fists.'"

"Thanks, O'Toole. Tell the boys I'm against the man who robs his woodsmen in the wanigans. Tell them I'm against the man who would steal away their chance to get justice. Tell them I know Zaanan Frame is their best friend, and beg them to vote for him."

"Have no worries about the b'ys wid corked boots," said O'Toole. "Think ye we don't know Mike Moran?"

"But Zaanan won't help himself," said the old man.

"I'll see Zaanan the minute we get to town," promised Jim.

He kept his word. From the train he walked straight to Zaanan's office. Dolf Springer sat on the door-step, his head hunched down between his shoulders, a very picture of disconsolation. He scarcely looked up as Jim passed him.

Zaanan, as always in his leisure moments, was reading Tiffany's *Justices' Guide*. Jim fancied that the old man's figure was less erect than formerly, that it drooped with discouragement, with disappointment over the crumbling of the work of his life. Jim could mark on Zaanan's face the effects of the blow he had received when it became plain his people were turning against him. To realize their ingratitude, how little they appreciated the expenditure of his life in their behalf, must have grieved the old justice sorely.

He greeted Jim with his usual brief phrase, "Howdy?"

"Judge," said Jim, breaking impetuously into the subject of his coming, wasting no time in preliminaries, "we've got to get up and stir ourselves."

"Um! What's been happenin' to you now? Worried 'cause you couldn't sell your option?"

Jim was a bit startled at Zaanan's knowledge of the failure of his errand, but brushed aside his curiosity to know how the old justice came by his information.

"It's not myself I'm worrying about; it's you, Judge, and Diversity. Even your friends admit you're beaten. They say you admit it yourself. They think you're too old to get out and fight."

"Heard me admittin' I was beat, Jim, eh? Heard me sayin' any sich thing?"

"No."

"Think I'm too old, Jim, eh? Past my usefulness?"

"You're the best man of all of us. That's why—"

Zaanan's eyes twinkled for a moment, then he bent his head in an attitude of weariness, "Folks is tired of me, Jim. They calc'late I've outstayed my welcome. Noticed that, Jim, eh?"

"They've been bamboozled into thinking it, or paid to think it."

"But they think it, all the same. Any reason I shouldn't give 'em a chance to run their logs without me? See why I shouldn't git a minnit's peace and quiet at the tail end of my life, eh? Specially when folks is anxious I should?"

"Yes, Judge, I do see a reason. These are your people. You've made them what they are. You've looked after them for years and, maybe, because you've looked after them so thoroughly and well, they are less able to look after themselves than they should be. You're responsible for them. Nobody but you can save them and this town from passing into a condition that will be intolerable. You aren't entitled to rest. You've got to get into this fight—and win."

"Perty late, hain't it, Jim? Perty late in the day?"

"We'll just have to work that much harder."

"Dun'no's I kin agree with you, Jim. Seems to me time's too short. Maybe I should 'a' fought, but there wa'n't much encouragement. Folks was flockin' to Peleg. Shouldn't wonder if a dose of Peleg 'u'd be the thing to cure 'em."

"You mustn't leave them in the lurch. It's natural you should feel hard against them, but they-they've been fooled. It's not their fault."

"Somehow, Jim, I don't feel as able to undertake things as I did once." Zaanan's voice was weary, old. "Looks to me like it would be wastin' time to stir things up now. Calc'late I'm done for, Jim."

"All your friends haven't left you. But they need you to lead them. They don't know what to do."

"There hain't nothin' to do, Jim, against Moran and all his money."

"But won't you come out and try? Go down fighting, anyhow."

"Hain't no occasion for it, Jim. Better save up what strength I've got left. No use wastin' it in vain efforts."

A surge of sympathy for the old man welled up in Jim. Sitting there in the latter end of his days, deserted by friends, abandoned by those for whom he had striven for a score of years, he could not be contemplated unmoved. In his discouragement he was pitiful indeed.

"Judge," Jim said, impulsively, "I wish I could drop everything and jump into this thing for you. I can't do that, but I can do something. Until caucus day I'm going to give every possible minute to this election, whether you help or not."

"Much obleeged," said Zaanan, without enthusiasm. "What's your special int'rest in this thing, eh? Seems to me like you was consid'able wrought up over it."

Jim hesitated.

What was his interest? Was it merely hatred for Moran, or was it something worthier? He paused to search his soul for the answer.

"Before my father induced me to take over this business I had other plans. I had been a newspaper man in the city. I had seen things, and it seemed to me that there was room for somebody who wanted to help. The people—the people at the bottom of the heap—need help, Judge. They don't belong. They pay their dues in money or labor, but they're not members. They have none of the privileges. Perhaps they aren't entitled to the privileges; perhaps they wouldn't know what to do with them if they got them, but they're entitled to something. Our Declaration of Independence says something about all men being born free and equal. In theory that may be true. In practice only those are free and equal who are strong enough to force others to recognize their freedom and equality. I wanted to do something—one man could do only a little—toward helping the bottom of the heap out from under to where the weight of the top of the heap wouldn't crush them."

"Um! One of them newfangled socialists, eh?"

"I don't know. I don't know just what a socialist is, but if what I've said makes me one, then I'm guilty of the charge."

"Hain't jest normal for a feller employin' men and women like you do."

"That is one of the things that moved me to accept father's proposition when he turned things over to me. I could do my small part here. I could at least see that my bottom-heapers got a fair trade from me, who was their top-heaper. And I guess that's why I'm interested in this election. You've kept things spread out so the bottom was not smashed by the top. Moran wants to take your place so he can crush the bottom as he wants to."

"Um! No pers'nal spite?"

Jim flushed.

"I hate Moran."

"Not astonished to hear it. Now, abandonin' the election for a minute and takin' up your affairs: I bought me a couple shares in the Diversity Hardwood Company t'other day. Had the chance. Thought maybe you'd be wantin' to take 'em off my hands. Figgered you might find a use for 'em. Think you kin, eh? Annual meetin' of that corporation comes day follerin' caucus. Better git them shares properly transferred on the company's books right off. Here they be."

"But—" began Jim.

"Hain't I said them shares might come in handy? Paid two hundred dollars for 'em. Gimme check."

Zaanan's methods were now more or less familiar to Jim. He knew the justice would not have bought this stock for him without some good reason. He scented some plan that Zaanan was working out.

"All right, Judge."

"Git that transfer made right off."

"Without fail," said Jim.

"G'-by, Jim."

"Good afternoon, Judge. But I wish you—"

"G'-by, Jim," repeated Zaanan, with a convincing tone of finality.

From that day for the week that remained before the caucus Jim talked, argued, pleaded with the voters of Diversity. He even essayed public speaking; hired the local opera-house for the purpose, and there publicly denounced Peleg Goodwin as Moran's cat's-paw; publicly excoriated Moran. But he came to perceive his was a hopeless task.

He could not arouse the people. Zaanan himself might have stirred them, but no stranger could. Especially no stranger could stir them to fight for Zaanan when Zaanan himself acknowledged defeat.

Some there were who fought shoulder to shoulder with Jim. Dolf Springer did what was in him, and when he saw the futility of it his watery eyes grew more watery still. Dolf was faithful; Zaanan was his great man. His faith in the goodness of God was shaken.

Moran did not abate his exertions. He himself, his agents, his hirelings, traversed the township, the county. Ceaselessly they worked, and tirelessly, efficiently. Their faces wore no looks of discouragement; their bearing was jaunty. Any man with half a political eye could see the victory was theirs. On the eve of the caucus Jim grudgingly admitted it, too.

That night—the hour was not quite nine—the young man who was Grierson's assistant in the bookkeeping realm—his name was Newell—rushed up to Jim on the hotel piazza. Obviously he was in a state of high excitement.

"Mr. Ashe! Mr. Ashe!" he panted.

Jim drew him aside.

"What is it, Newell?" he asked.

"Crab Creek Trestle, Mr. Ashe. They're going to burn it to-night, so you can't get any more logs."

"How do you know? Who told you?"

"I don't know the man—tall, carried a gun under his arm."

"Gilders," said Jim to himself. It was sufficient verification for him if the warning came from that man. "All right, Newell. Go along about your business and keep your mouth shut."

Jim did not pause to determine the best course to follow. For him there was but one course—instant action. Without halt, without plan, without aid, he set out for Crab Creek. It was a trip to be taken afoot. No road led to the spot. Jim made for the railroad, sped down it toward the threatened spot.

CHAPTER XXII

Marie Ducharme was expecting Michael Moran. He had sent word he would see her that evening, and she, her heart numbed by the blow it had received, was inclined to welcome him. Her mood was one of recklessness, bred and nurtured by days and nights of brooding over the injustice of which she was the victim. She had spent her night of agony and struggle; had come down from the moonlit knoll strengthened, lifted up by a surrender to love, exalted by victory won over sordid temptations. She had come down with soul renewed, purified, with fresh aspirations, with tender hopes, with a sort of pitiful pride. The gates of her heart had not been opened to the love that gained admittance. She had heard it clamoring without, had striven to exclude it; but it had won past her barriers. Once within, she had fought with it, opposed it with all the strength of her will. When her capitulation came it was complete. And Jim Ashe's cruel accusation had been its reward.

Her moment of hysteria in the garden passed, gave place to sullenness, to dull, throbbing pain, to revolt. At first there had been amazed grief, terror, unbelief in the possibility of such a thing. It would not be true. Such a thing could not happen to her. Realization followed. That it had happened was past denial. In her supreme moment, her moment of confession to Jim, he had rejected her love, responded to it with scorn. She had laid low her pride for his sake, and he had trampled on it. There were moments when she fancied she hated him. These moments recurred more frequently. Grief gave way to anger. He had prated of love, of the trust, the beauty of love, and at the first shadow his love had not been trustful. He had denied her a hearing, condemned her before she could make defense; and as she had come to understand love, defenses were abhorrent to it. His heart, his instinct, should have held him steadfast in his faith. It had failed, so his love had failed. Then love was not what she had come to believe.

She had told Jim her love would be a fiery thing, jealous, demanding. She had seen it so; but now she knew love was not of that warp and woof. The joy of love was in service, in surrender. It lay not in compelling service of its object, but in rendering service to him. In that spirit she had gone to Jim; and how had he received her?

So she believed she hated him. Also, as she tried to peer ahead, she saw a future without peace, troubled, dark. If it were to be so, what was the use of further struggle? In the old days she had contemplated without abhorrence a deliberate choice of the lower course. Now she fondled the suggestion. If that way had pleasure, life, joys, no matter how spurious, why should she not take them? Life owed her something. Hitherto it had withheld; latterly it had ruthlessly heaped woe upon her. Why not reach out and seize whatever the world had to give? It would entail pain, perhaps. But would that be harder to bear than what lay ahead if she held steadfast in the course she had chosen? Love had come—and gone. It would not renew its coming. Such was her judgment.

Moran came, sat beside her. He was agitated, not wholly by his feeling for her, but by rage, jealousy, vindictiveness which he burned to vent on Jim Ashe. When he spoke, that gentler note which he had used in talking to her on former occasions was absent from his voice; it was harsh, strained. Marie sat numb, silent, shivering a trifle. She was conscious of a physical repulsion for the man; conscious she would be compelled to pay a price exorbitant for the toys she hoped to buy.

"Marie," said Moran, "you've dallied with me. You've held me off. You've pretended not to understand me when I knew you understood, when it was plain you did understand. And I've been patient—because a man must be a fool when he deals with women. You're no child. You know what you want. You know I can give it to you. When are you going to make up your mind?"

"When I am ready to make up my mind. When I know what I want."

"You know now. It's just the infernal woman in you that wants to toy with a man. I'm no man to be toyed with—past a safe point. I'd have been contented to play your game a little longer if it hadn't been for old Frame's meddling."

"Judge Frame? What meddling?"

Moran shrugged his shoulders angrily.

"Don't talk as if you thought I was an imbecile. What meddling? Don't you suppose I knew why old Frame sent that man Ashe here?" At mention of Jim's name Marie winced.

"Why did Judge Frame—"

"To marry you," said Moran, his tone brutal as a blow. "And you knew it. You've been playing Ashe against me—to see which of us you could get the most from. You've landed Ashe high and dry—anybody can see that. It's my business to see Ashe doesn't land you."

Jealousy showed there. Marie flinched as though Moran touched an exposed nerve.

"I hate him! I hate him!" she cried.

"Hate him or love him, it don't matter. He sha'n't have you. I've fixed that. After to-night—to-morrow—you won't want him if you want him now. Maybe you hate him. I'm not fool enough to believe it because you say so. It don't matter. I don't care who you love or hate, so long as I have you. I'd have smashed him, anyhow. That was business. But he's shoved in between you and me, and I'll smash him and stamp on him. It's as good as done. And Frame—he'll be disposed of to-morrow." His voice was rising, becoming shrill as he fanned his passion.

Marie felt the stirring of some emotion within her. It was apprehension, fear. Even in that moment she could scrutinize it as something outside herself, wonder at it. Why was she apprehensive? She was not afraid for herself. For whom was she afraid? She must be afraid for Jim Ashe, for he was the threatened man. It was unbelievable. She told herself she did not, could not, care what befell Jim Ashe. She hated him, despised him.

"You may as well cast Ashe out of your reckoning," Moran went on. "There'll be nothing to reckon on. I know what you want—money. Money to buy excitement, movement, money to throw away, money to buy for you everything Diversity can't give. I know. Well, Ashe will have trouble giving you a decent meal in another twenty-four hours."

"I do hate him!" Marie said, aloud, but to herself. "I do! I do!"

"Then you'll be glad to hear his stay in Diversity is coming to a sudden end."

Here was a threat which it seemed to her touched Jim's own person, his safety. Marie uttered a scarce audible gasp. "Jim?" she whispered. "No.... No.... Not that. Not Jim." In that instant she knew her fear was for Jim, a living, chilling fear. If fear lived, then love must live, too. She did not hate him; she had lied to herself, deceived herself. No matter how he had wronged her, no matter how he had judged her, she loved him. And she was glad, glad, for it rekindled her faith in human love. Love should forgive all, suffer all. And she loved with such a love. It was good.

"I'm through waiting for your whims," Moran said. "What I want I take. I've put him out of the way. I've made it necessary for you to come to me. To-morrow you'll be told you aren't needed here any more."

"What?" said Marie.

"You'll teach no more school in Diversity. You've hated it. Well, I saw to that."

She did not know if what he said were fact or threat.

It did not matter. Moran had made his big mistake, for hers was not a will to brook threat. If more was needed to array her actively against him, he had contributed what was needed.

In the gloom of the porch he could not see the transformation that took place in her; could not see that a different woman sat opposite him—a woman alert, full of the wiles that from time immemorial have been the weapon of women, a woman to fear. The numbness that had clung to her, oppressed her—a heavy fog obscuring the world—was wafted away in an instant, as a fog on her own Lake Michigan dissipated, disappeared before morning breeze and morning sun. She sat there, not Marie Ducharme crushed, ready for any fate that promised a measure of kindliness, but Marie Ducharme with youth and love in her heart—youth and love, and fear for the man she loved.

And there was something else. There was the will to fight for the love that was hers; the will to win again what she had lost. It was not right, fair, that she should lose. It was error. She did not even blame Jim now. She was given to see that the words he had spoken to her lacerated his own heart more than they lacerated hers. Opposite Michael Moran sat Marie Ducharme, fighting with all the force and the gifts that were in her for the man she loved.

She moved forward in her chair, leaned a little toward Moran.

"You—you have a will," she said.

Moran saw her weakening. It had been a perfect thing, not too apparent, convincing.

"You're through backing and filling," he said, stating it as a fact, not asking it as a question.

"And you're sure—sure you can do what you say, to him?"

He glanced at her quickly, astonished at the vindictiveness that cut through her words.

"What's he been doing to you?" he asked, jocularly.

"Enough. No matter. He—he can't avoid it? You know you can do as you say—crush him?"

"I wouldn't care to have you get a spite against me, young lady. Yes, I've got him—so." He closed his hand tightly. "It's a matter of business, with you added to make it more interesting. I'm here to make money, and I'm going to make some of it out of Ashe—so much, in fact, that he won't have any left. And that's interesting to you, isn't it? From now on he's going to learn something about business."

"But," she said, "he's had the best of you, hasn't he?"

"He bragged of that, eh? I'll admit he had more gumption than I figured on, but he's gone his limit. I'm taking personal charge now. He's in deep water, Marie. He's up against a hard fight in his own line, bucking a combination. They've put prices down to where he loses money on every clothespin he makes.

"He's in deep—borrowed money all over the shop, and no way to pay it. To-night will end his thrashing round. Can't run without logs."

"Yes," Marie said, setting a thorn into Moran's skin, "but he's getting logs. Didn't he take your logging-road away from you?"

"But he won't run it any longer. You know where Crab Creek Trestle is? Well, the logs are all on the other side of it. And they're going to stay there. The Diversity Hardwood Company is going to have the misfortune to lose its trestle by fire to-night. He'll have to shut down. Then creditors will get worried. They'll be down on him, but I'll be there a little ahead."

"How?" said Marie, breathlessly.

"I'm a director of the Diversity Bank," he chuckled. "Ashe borrowed thirty thousand dollars of us, and gave a demand-note. You know what that is?"

"Yes."

"To-morrow the note will be presented. He'll have to raise that amount of money inside of three days—and he can't do it. Oh, it won't be long before a man named Michael Moran will be manufacturing clothespins with Ashe's machinery."

"But if you should fail about the trestle, if it shouldn't burn, would he be able to beat you and keep his mill?"

Moran shrugged his shoulders.

"Possibly, but there's no use thinking about that, The trestle is as good as gone."

"Oh!" said Marie, and sank back in her chair.

It was so complete, so perfect. Jim was beaten. He had worked so hard, so faithfully; had builded such high hopes—to go down in ruin! Jim! And nothing she could do or say would stay the disaster, would postpone it an instant. She shivered, coughed.

"It's cold. A moment while I get my shawl."

She stepped into the house. Moran waited, warmed by a feeling of complete satisfaction. She was his; at last she had surrendered. And Ashe was in the hollow of his hand. Zaanan Frame, too, was beaten.

From first to last the thing had been handled efficiently, as an able business man should handle it. He leaned back and lighted a cigar.

For a few moments he puffed contentedly. Marie did not return. Presently he grew impatient. Another few minutes, and he leaped up to tramp the length of the porch.

Still she did not come. He stepped to the door and called:

"Marie! Marie! What's keeping you all this time?"

There was no answer. He called again, went inside. Marie was not downstairs. He called Mrs. Stickney. The widow answered from above.

"Is Marie up there?" Moran called.

"Hain't seen her," said the widow.

"Didn't she just come up there?"

"Not unless she's quieter'n a spook. Nobody's passed my door."

"Where is she, then?" He was in a rage now. "Where's she gone to?"

"I hain't no idee," said the widow, sharply, "but if she's where you don't know where she is I calc'late I'm satisfied."

Her door slammed. Moran stood an instant. The suspicion that had been germinating within him became certainty. The girl had played him like a fish. She was gone to warn Ashe.

He pulled his hat on furiously and ran—ran toward the hotel to intercept Marie.

CHAPTER XXIII

Marie stopped, panting, at the hotel piazza. "Mr. Ashe?" she said. "Where's Mr. Ashe?"

"Hain't been gone more 'n couple of minutes. Feller, all excited up, stopped and says somethin' to him, and off he goes like somebody was robbin' his hen-house."

She was too late! He was gone! Where? Marie guessed. Somebody else had warned him, and he was off for Crab Creek Trestle.

"Who was with him? Did he go alone?"

"Just up and rushed off like sixty. Didn't wait for nothin' or nobody."

It was like him. Sudden Jim! He had not paused for help, but had plunged ahead alone. How futile it was! What could he do alone save rush into danger? Marie felt there was danger. A business matter Moran had called it, yet in the heart of the woods that might happen which could not be considered a business transaction. Jim might come upon Moran's agents as they set their fire. What then? Would they pause to consider if here were business? Would Jim pause to think of business? No. There would be violence—and Jim alone.

There is a cave-dweller hidden in each of us. At some hour it will emerge, our varnish of civilization will peel from us, and we shall stand forth primitive, thinking, functioning as did the remote ancestors of the race. This was Marie's hour. Her man was rushing into danger—and she was not with him.

She did not consider if her presence would help; if she could do better service otherwise. Her instinct was to be with him, to share what came to him. She would warn him, delay him, if possible. But that was not the chief thing. The foremost thought was to stand at his side, to feel his presence.

Unconscious of the stares of astonishment that followed her, the buzz of comment and surmise that remained behind, she followed the path Jim had taken, heading toward the railroad. But she did not follow the rails as Jim had done. She crossed the track and plunged into a marshy country, treacherous underfoot, grown thickly with undergrowth that tore at her garments, scratched her face. She was cutting across a curve in the railroad, hoping so to overtake Jim.

Now she floundered and fell, was up again to struggle forward. Her feet sank in marsh ooze; sometimes she waded stagnant water that gurgled above her shoe-tops. But she stopped for nothing. Another might have become confused in the blackness of the night, for the moon was hidden by clouds which promised storm, but Marie had traversed those woods again and again. She was the daughter of a lumberjack, and woodcraft was bred into the very fiber of her.

Once her ankle turned under her with a sickening pain; but she forced herself to rise and limp onward. "Hurry! Hurry! Hurry!" she whispered to herself over and over again, unconscious that she was whispering. Her body was not inured to such endeavors, but her will was master of her body. When exhaustion would have brought her to the ground her will held her upright, gave her strength to flounder onward, always to the accompaniment of that hysterical whisper: "Hurry! Hurry! Hurry!"

Her skirts, soggy with the slime of marsh pools, clung to her legs; her hair hung about her face, caught on projecting branches, to be torn loose ruthlessly. She seemed not to feel the pain of it. The flesh of her hands was lacerated; blood oozed from more than one abrasion upon her cheeks. She was unconscious of it. All of consciousness that remained was the knowledge that Jim Ashe was there ahead of her somewhere, going to his death, perhaps; that she could, must warn him, save him So she floundered on, with the whispered words "Hurry! Hurry! Hurry!" urging her ahead. Perhaps she heard the words; perhaps they helped to spur her on. There came a moment when she did hear them, but fancied they were spoken by another. "Hurry! Hurry! Hurry!"

It seemed as if she had been traveling so always, forcing her way through nightmare obstructions, encountering such vain labors as are only to be met with in vivid, horrible dreams. Then she tripped, fell, striking her shoulder against something hard, cold. She felt it with her hand, and cried aloud. It was the railroad! She had won to the railroad!

Was Jim ahead or behind? There was no time to study. Her mind was in no condition to reason; there was only the feverish urge that forced her on. "Hurry! Hurry! Hurry!" She turned up the track, now trying pitifully to run, now wavering, staggering, but always persevering.

How black it was! She strained her eyes forward. He might be near, very near, yet she could not see him, and any moment her strength might fail.

She demanded yet another effort from the forces so near exhaustion. "Jim!" she cried, shrilly, wildly. "Jim! Jim! Wait, oh, wait!"

A hundred yards up the track Jim heard the cry, stopped, listened.

"Jim, wait!" It sounded more faintly. A woman's voice, here, calling his name! There was but one woman in Diversity who had ever called him Jim.

In this moment, a moment he knew was weighted with danger to him, came her voice out of the black mystery that lay behind him. It was startling, unbelievable. He asked himself if much worry, much travail of heart, had not deranged some spring or cog in his imagination, so that he heard things which were not. If it really were Marie, what was she doing there? She had betrayed him once; was this another act in tune with her betrayal? He braced himself against a fresh danger, an unforeseen danger, and waited.

She tottered up to him out of the black blanket of night; tottered, hands fumbling before her, his name on her lips, his name and that other word which her will had set there so that it was repeated endlessly without volition: "Jim, hurry! Hurry! Hurry!"

Her fingers touched him before she was aware of his presence; touched him, clung to him. She cried aloud, inarticulately. Panting, sobbing, she tried to speak, but only repeated over and over that one word: "Hurry! Hurry! Hurry!"

He felt her fingers slipping from him, felt her body sagging, falling. His arm passed round her, sustaining her. Her head sank in the hollow of her arm and she sighed with weary contentment.

"Marie, what is it?"

"Hurry!" she muttered.

But he shook her, not roughly, but with boyish impatience, boyish alarm.

"No, no! Why are you here? What is the matter?"

Her mind cleared slowly; her will that had set on one determination, to reach him—set so it could not loose its hold—relaxed. She breathed deeply, pushed against him in an effort to stand free.

"Crab Creek Trestle," she said. "He's—going to burn it. He warned you—to get you—out here."

His suspicion reared itself between them.

"How do you know? What are you doing here? Did he send you?"

She quivered, sobbed dryly—then she shoved him away.

"I know because he boasted of it. That—and other things. To-morrow that—note. The bank will make you pay it. He—said he—would be making clothespins—in your mill—"

"But you—why are you here? What do you want?"

She summoned her strength and her pride.

"It doesn't—matter why—I am here. You must go back. You mustn't go on."

"So that's it," he said, bitterly. "He sent you to hold me back till they could do the work."

He turned and began to stride away.

"No!" she cried. "You mustn't go!"

"Go back to town, Marie," he said, his voice quivering, not with wrath, but with pain. "Go back. I'm going on."

"You mustn't!" She took one tottering step toward him and sank until she was on her knees. He would not believe her. He would not be warned.

What she had suffered, the things she had just done, had been in vain.

"Go back," he said, dully. "It isn't safe out there. Go back."

"It isn't safe for you—for *you*. It's planned to have you come—alone."

He moved away from her. She forced herself to rise.

"Then I'll go with you," she said.

"Go back!" he commanded.

"No," she said, and tottered on.

He set his teeth, turned his face away from her, and went on, unmindful of her sobbing, gasping breaths. At one moment they saw a redness in the sky; saw the darkness ahead fluttering like a waved cloth.

"Fire," Jim muttered, and began to run. He was too late—Crab Creek Trestle was in names!

As best she could Marie followed. He gained, but she did not falter, urged herself to her utmost. Ahead of them the trestle came into view, wreathed in flames, flames that leaped and writhed and strained upward as if seeking to be released from bonds that held them to earth. The trees and bushes about seemed to rise and fall with the swelling of the tongues of fire. In the midst the framework of the trestle stood black, stark, startlingly vivid.

For a moment Jim stood where bank and trestle met, stood undecided. There was nothing to do, yet he must do something, for it was his nature to do something. Nothing would save the trestle. He perceived that, though he hesitated to admit it. He saw that the work of incendiarism had been done efficiently; timbers had been well soaked with oil, and the match applied not in one spot but in scores of places. Except for a matter of thirty feet at the end where Jim stood the whole structure was flame-wrapped.

From the very brook fire seemed to flow upward; here and there, twenty feet below, marsh grass burst into ruddy, living flower.

Without plan or reason Jim started forward upon the trestle, as if to plunge headlong into the dancing, undulating, seething mass of destruction and stifle it with his hands.

Marie, now at his side, clutched his arm to restrain him. He shook her off ungently, sprang forward. She kept at his side. Again he was forced to pause, shading his face from the heat that reached out to meet him. His eyes were for nothing but the fire; saw nothing aside from it.

Waves of heat surged against him, forced him to draw back, and the very action of retreating cleared his head, restored him to something resembling calm. Instinct, impulse withdrew, leaving intellect in command. He thought of his father. What he saw before him was his father's—Clothespin Jimmy's—life-work disappearing in flames. He had been given his father's shoes. How had he filled them? The destruction of this trestle was the destruction of the Ashe Clothespin Company. He should have foreseen this danger, guarded against it adequately. In that he had failed.

Again Marie was at his side. "Come back," she said. "You can do no good."

He did not notice her, but stepped forward again, forcing himself against the heat. She clung to him.

"You can't put it out," she said again. "Come back out of danger."

He turned on her, eyes flashing, jaw set.

"Put it out!" he said, harshly. "I'm not thinking about putting it out. It's gone!" He was Sudden Jim now, not defeated, still fighting.

"Go back and tell Moran you left me figuring how to get logs from there to here. And tell him I'm going to do it. Tell him if he'd burned the woods I'd find some way to make logs out of the ashes."

Presently he spoke again—to himself.

"I wish Nelson was here," he said. He was trying to figure construction, needed his millwright's advice.

In that moment Clothespin Jimmy might have felt satisfaction in his son, for young Jim had forgotten the blow just dealt him, had forgotten the fire that raged at his feet. His thoughts dealt only with the future. He wasted no moment in discouragement, though he might well have been discouraged. One thought he held: Logs must cross the gap before him. But how? His fingers doubled into determined fists.

"It can be done," he said, "and I'll find the way!"

An older woodsman than Jim, a man experienced in the handling of logs, would have shaken his head. Such a man would have seen the difficulties of the task; would have declared it impossible to haul timber across that swamp before winter.

Jim's inexperience refused to be daunted.

His head was clear now; he was himself. Marie—she had been there. He turned upon her.

"What are you doing here?" he demanded, fiercely, but she was not upright before him. She lay upon the cross-ties, one arm dangling limply through, the garish light exaggerating the pallor of her face.

"Marie!" he whispered, hoarsely.

She did not stir or answer. Her endurance had been urged to the point of breakage, had given way. He was on his knees beside her, his heart gripped by fear, for he had never seen a woman faint. He lifted her. Her head lopped grotesquely to one side as he moved her, and this multiplied his fright. He had loved her, and she was dead. She had not been worth a man's love; had been treacherous; had betrayed him; but he had given her all of his love. Her breast lifted laboriously. He was conscious of a feeling of relief, not of gladness. So this would not be the end of things between them. They would continue to inhabit the same world. To him it seemed the world was oversmall to house them both.

Whatever she had done, he could not leave her so. He strained until she lay partly across his shoulder—a weight it would have been joy for him to bear a few short hours before—and so, staggering under his burden, he strove toward Diversity.

Long miles lay between him and town; no help was nearer; no shelter for Marie. He found himself near the point of exhaustion. But he labored on.

After a length of time that seemed to have stretched into hours Jim was aware of the dark figure of a man standing between the tracks before him.

Somehow Jim was not interested in it, was not interested in anything save the effort to keep on his feet and make progress. The man spoke with a voice Jim knew but did not identify.

"Who are you?" Jim asked, in a whisper.

"Gilders," said the man. "Here, I'll take her. You carry my rifle. You've lugged her about as far as you can, hain't you?"

"All of that," Jim said, surrendering his burden and sitting down abruptly.

"Rest a bit," said Gilders. "When you're ready, say so. We'll take her to my place—it's nearer 'n Diversity."

Presently Jim got to his feet.

"All right," he said.

Gilders raised Marie without effort and strode away with her in his arms. Jim followed. At times Gilders waited to permit Jim to rest, for Jim could not equal the woodsman's pace, indeed could not have sustained any pace at all without frequent stops.

That last tramp was a thing of vagueness to Jim. How long it was, how many minutes, hours, days it required to traverse the distance, he did not know. It was a hades of blackness and weariness and pain. At last they arrived at Gilders's shanty. Steve laid Marie on his bed. Jim waited for no bed, but sank to the floor, and the night held no further consciousness for him.

Somehow Steve procured a neighbor woman who gave of her kindliness and skill to Marie, ministering, watching through the night. Steve let Jim lie as he had fallen. Sleep, he knew, would work its own reviving miracle.

CHAPTER XXIV

On caucus days or election days it had been Zaanan Frame's custom to sit in his office and receive his friends. There were few who did not take that opportunity to shake Zaanan's hand, to show themselves at his levee. Most came because it was their pleasure to do so; some came because they regarded it as the part of wisdom.

But on this caucus day Zaanan sat alone. Outside on the steps was Dolf Springer, taciturn, doleful. That was all. The old man was deserted. Diversity had forsaken him on the day of his downfall. The power he had wielded for more than a generation had dropped from him, leaving in the place of the political dictator merely a tired, weary, disappointed old man.

He had taken some comfort in that greatest of all books, the *Justices' Guide*. Now he laid it aside and rose.

"Dolf," he called.

The one faithful retainer entered.

"Calc'late we'll be startin' for the op'ry-house, Dolf."

On other years this had been a sort of triumphal procession. Zaanan had marched to the opera-house surrounded by his friends. Now he looked quizzically at Dolf.

"Seems like we was sort of scarce this mornin', Dolf, eh?"

"Doggone 'em!" said Dolf, vindictively.

They started, a pitiful procession. As they made their progress there were eyes that turned away with a feeling of shame; other eyes stared gleefully. Here was ocular evidence that Zaanan Frame was beaten; that they, the sovereign voters of Diversity, had been able thus easily to reach out and pluck him down.

When Zaanan arrived the opera-house was full. Zaanan, who had for years been given a conspicuous place of honor, found a seat with difficulty. He sank listlessly into his chair, slid forward with extended legs, and let the brush of his beard rest on the bosom of his shirt. He did not look about him.

Had he studied the hall, he must have been surprised, not alone at the numbers present, but at the composition of the spectators. In Diversity women were accustomed to take no part in politics—even that slight part of watching their men functioning in caucus or convention. But this morning was presented a condition abnormal. The gallery, usually occupied by a sprinkling of loafers, was filled with women. Not ten women or a score of women, but row after row of women; the mothers and wives of Diversity in a body.

Others had been surprised by it. Not a few husbands had remarked upon it to wives as they left their housework and departed. Some wives had evaded questions; the bolder ones and the majority did not hesitate to inform their husbands, in words easily understood, that their reasons for going to the caucus were nobody's business but their own.

The monotonous routine of organization was completed. Throughout, Peleg Goodwin had been in the public eye. He was a figure of importance. He already assumed the dignity of the office which was to be his as it had once been Zaanan's. Peleg had views as to his future. What Zaanan had done Peleg could do. True, Moran was putting him where he was; but later—Peleg would see to that. His bearing was feudal.

The gallery had watched impatiently, if silently. So this was politics? So these futilely buzzing, smoking, lounging male creatures below were actually their husbands exercising a high rite of citizenship! It was monotonous. It even moved some of them to giggles. Many of them had invested the caucus with the dignity of mystery, with a certain pomp and regality. Now they saw it as it was, in no wise different from a casual gathering round the wood-stove in the post-office on any day in winter.

"So that's how it's done," said the Widow Stickney. "Huh! 'Tain't much more glitterin' than peelin' potaters. And I doubt if it's as useful."

But when the moment arrived for nominations for the office of justice of the peace, the women leaned forward, interested, not to miss a phase of it.

Young Lawyer Bourne placed Peleg in nomination, did so noisily, flamboyantly, with waving of arms and screaming of eagle. He mentioned Peleg as Peleg had never been mentioned before. If the young man had not mentioned Peleg's name at the outset, that worthy candidate would not himself have recognized the subject of the speech. But Peleg enjoyed it. Maybe that's what he really was and hadn't realized it; maybe that's what his fellow-men had been thinking about him for years, wasted years. Why, with such regard he might have risen to the Governor's chair!

"Look at Peleg," whispered the widow. "If somebody don't tie a strap round his chist he's a-goin' to bust."

Peleg's nomination was duly seconded, not by Michael Moran, for Moran's residence was elsewhere, but to Moran's satisfaction. He sat on the aisle, well toward the front, and had been the recipient of much attention. Easily

Moran was the dominant figure of the body. Why should he not be, on this his day of victory over his enemies?

Zaanan sat motionless, spoke to no one, paid no attention to what went forward. He was there, that was all. It seemed as if he had come from, habit, not from interest. After the first few moments he was forgotten, unnoticed. Zaanan had been moved on to oblivion.

Bob Allen nominated Zaanan. He made no speech, simply mounted the platform and announced that he placed the name of Zaanan Frame before the caucus as a candidate for the justiceship. It was a form, that was all. Then he stepped down.

"Any secondin' speech?" asked the chairman—a form, too.

"Calc'late there is," said a voice at the rear of the hall, and Steve Gilders arose, for once detached from the rifle which had grown to be as much a part of him as his arms.

As Steve walked forward, indeed, as the first of his words fell on the ears of the body, it became silent. Men looked at one another, felt a tenseness in the air, an apprehension. A small boy walked by Steve's side, his hand in Steve's.

Together they mounted the platform, stood facing the hall.

"I'm here to second that there nomination," Steve said, harshly. "Bein's I haint taught in speech-makin' I fetched help. But I figger the boy and me'll be able to make out."

He got down on one knee so his face was on a level with the child's.

"What's your name?" he asked.

"Steve," said the little one.

"What's your other name?"

"Hain't got none."

Every man, every woman, in the house was straining forward. Here was something not to be expected by any; something fraught with meaning. Michael Moran was of those whose eyes were fixed on the two figures. He half arose to his feet, then sank back, face distorted, fists clenched.

"Who was your ma?" Steve asked, in a voice that chilled.

"Susie Gilders."

"Where is she?"

"She's dead."

"What killed her?"

"She did," said the child, his lips quivering.

"Why?"

"On account of me."

The gallery became audible—it gasped once, then was silent again.

"Who is your pa?" Steve went on, inexorably.

"Michael Moran."

"Who do you hate?"

"Michael Moran."

Steve arose, lifted the child above his head.

"Look at him, folks," he said; "he's secondin' the nomination of Zaanan Frame."

He turned, now leading the boy, descended from the platform, passed down the aisle toward the rear of the hall. The child's coat brushed Moran's sleeve, unconscious of whom it passed. Moran shrank away from the touch.

Nobody spoke, nobody moved, save Moran. He leaped to his feet, face working with rage, with shame, with the ignominy of it.

"It's a lie!" he shouted.

"It's the truth!" Steve Gilders said over his shoulder.

In the gallery a woman stood. She pointed downward to an individual on the floor.

"Tom Samson," she said, shrilly, "you're goin' to vote now. Vote right or don't come home to me."

Another woman dared equally. "You, too, George Perkins."

Woman after woman was on her feet, singling out her man, letting him hear her voice in this matter.

The vote was taken in silence, counted in silence. The hall awaited its announcement in silence. Three votes were cast for Peleg Goodwin, the rest for Zaanan Frame.

There was a cheer, but it came not from the floor, not from the men folk. It was shriller than a cheer by the men would have been, for it came from the throats of the wives and mothers of them. Women not accustomed to politics had taken a hand in that game. Women not granted the suffrage by our laws had by their mere presence wielded the powers of the suffrage. They had not voted in person for Zaanan Frame; they had exerted no prior influence; but they had at the moment of action shown their men what was in their hearts, and the men voted in accord with it. The women of Diversity had shown there was a force, a power resident within them, that was capable of ruling when it sought to rule. Men versed in the law tell us that in every state the supreme power must lie definitely in some individual or some group of individuals. Where autocracy, absolutism, obtains, the supreme fountainhead of authority is in the autocrat; in a republic it abides in the citizens. The women of Diversity had made apparent where resided the ultimate authority in their village.

Moran had left the opera-house.

Scatteringly at first, then with volume, arose shouts for Zaanan. Shamefaced men bellowed his name, at first because they were ashamed, afraid, to do otherwise, then with an infection of enthusiasm, perhaps with a clearness of vision they had been deprived of hitherto. Zaanan walked forward slowly, gravely, with no indication of elation in his face. From the platform he eyed them sternly.

"Folks," he began, presently, "I can't say I take any pride in this. I don't feel like I'd been honored. No, I hain't been honored, except by them that hadn't votes to vote. My heart hain't so old but it kin appreciate bein' trusted and respected by them that sits in the gallery. They stayed by me when you forsook me. You men, 'tain't on your accounts I'm takin' this place agin; it's because of them women that I've seen babies in their cradles, and for the babies that is in their cradles to-day."

He stopped to remove his spectacles.

"I should 'a' let you have a dose of Peleg and Moran. It would 'a' been good for you. But I seen you didn't have sense nor judgment to know what you was doin', so I done what I've had to do before. I took things into my own hands, and for another spell things'll go on as they did before. I was hopin' you'd learned. I was hopin', when I come to step out for good, that you'd be fit to handle the job yourselves. I'm disapp'inted in that, so I'll hang on as long as I can."

He stopped again and tugged at his beard, and glowered at the men as one might glower at refractory children.

"Some of you men that's here to-day has money in your pockets that don't b'long there. It's Michael Moran's money. For a dollar or two, that'll be spent and forgot in a week, you sold somethin' that's next worse to sell than the decency of your homes. You sold somethin' that men have fought for and give their all for. The whole of this here nation's built up on you and others like you. You're a part of the Gov'ment; the nation trusts each feller to do his votin' and his politics to the best of his judgment. But you hain't done that. You've up and sold your votes. I calc'late I hain't never been more ashamed. At the door of this op'ry-house is Dolf Springer holdin' a bushel basket. He's holdin' it in plain sight of all. If you that's took money hopes to have my respect, and the respect of your wives and mothers and daughters, you'll rise now and march past Dolf, and you'll chuck into that basket the Judas-money that's soilin' your pockets. Now, I'm waitin'."

They looked at one another shamefaced, each man afraid to be the first to rise.

"Tom Samson," came his wife's voice, "you head that percession."

There was the hint of a nervous laugh from the men, but Tom got to his feet.

"Zaanan," he said, shakily, "I'm a dum sight more ashamed 'n you be of me," and he marched to make his deposit in Dolf's basket.

It was a procession. Men formed in line behind Tom, and there were leathery faces that felt for the first time in many years the down-trickle of tears. Zaanan was wiping his eyes unashamed. Audible sobs descended from the gallery. The atmosphere was that of a revival—it was a revival, a moment of regeneration, a moment that would linger in the minds of those men as long as mind and body remained bound together. The line filed past Dolf and the men returned to their seats.

"I calc'late the business of this caucus is about over," Zaanan said. "When what's left to be done is over I wisht Parson Bloom 'u'd say a benediction. 'Tain't usual at sich meetin's, but 'twon't do any harm."

So it was done. Aged Parson Bloom mounted the platform, his silvery head bared, and held his arms extended over them. His words were few, simple:

"'The Lord watch between me and thee, when we are absent one from another.'"

Then they passed out, leaving Zaanan alone on the platform, seated in a huge arm-chair, his head bent wearily, his face in his hands.

CHAPTER XXV

Jim, in what might be termed a ramshackle physical condition, drove to town the morning of the caucus. His left arm occupied a sling. He had not seen Marie. She would not have known him had he seen her, for she lay in the borderland, not delirious, not unconscious wholly, but strangely indifferent, still. He did not wish to see her.

He went directly to his office, nor did he leave it during the morning. The caucus was in progress. He had been vitally interested in it. But this morning nothing interested him; he was apathetic. Part of this was due to physical condition, more to mental stress.

Even when the Diversity Bank presented for payment his note for thirty thousand dollars he was not aroused. It would have been his nature to do something, anything, in an effort to avert calamity; but it was not Sudden Jim who sat before his desk. It was just Jim, shorn of the attribute which had earned him his name.

He had expected the note to be presented. Well, he could not pay. There was no way to pay. Somehow he had failed, and his father would think the family blood had grown thin in his veins. Even that mattered little. Moran had beaten him. The burning of Crab Creek Trestle was a decisive blow. Before it could be replaced the logs in his yard would be exhausted, the mills must shut down for lack of raw material. There was no use to try to sweep back the inevitable; it was attempting to stay the inflowing tide with a broom.

He did not leave the office at dinner-time, but asked young Newell to fetch him a lunch from the hotel. Three days remained, the days of grace allowed by law after the presentation of his note. He saw no use for them.

It had not yet struck one o'clock when Zaanan Frame came in.

"Feelin' perty bad, Jim, eh? Had a perty tough time?"

Jim nodded.

"Git on your hat. I've fetched Tiffany, and we'll drive down to the Diversity Company's annual meetin'. Guess a drive after the best hoss in the county'll perk you up consid'able."

"What's the use, Judge? They've got me. I'm done."

"Huh! Sudden Jim, eh? Don't act very sudden jest now. What's ailin' your ambition?"

Jim told him briefly, with complete discouragement.

"Wasn't at the caucus this mornin'?" Zaanan asked.

"No; I didn't have the heart to go."

"Figgered I was beat, didn't you, eh? Figgered the ol' man didn't have a ghost of a show?"

"I knew it."

"Um! No more show 'n you've got to pull out of this mess? Not any more show than that, eh?"

"I guess we're in the same boat."

"You hain't asked who got nominated this mornin', Jim."

"No need to, Zaanan."

Zaanan chuckled. "Wa-al, you're a-goin' to hear news then. Peleg he slipped up some on his calc'lations."

Interest gleamed in Jim's eyes at last.

"What's that?" he said.

"Folks sort of, after a manner, made up their minds they couldn't git along without me."

"You beat them?"

"To be sure. And I hadn't no more chance 'n you've got. I was as beat as you be, if not beater, wasn't I? Which p'ints out the fact you never can tell who's licked till the constable stops the fight—and sometimes not then. Goin' to git on your hat, Jim?"

"Judge Frame," said Jim, "you're a great man! if you say to keep up the struggle, why"—he put on his hat and stood up—"why, let's get to that meeting."

"Hain't no time to lose. Got to git there swift, so I fetched Tiffany. You're goin' to ride behind a hoss now, young feller."

Jim did not smile.

Zaanan was not joking, but speaking with firm faith in his ancient steed. What Tiffany had been in his youth Tiffany still was to the old judge. The horse had not changed in his eyes. They had grown old together, but Zaanan's love for the creature, his admiration for qualities long vanished, were steadfast as ever.

"Lemme tell you some facts," said Zaanan. "There's times when facts is better ammunition 'n bullets. Moran's consid'able spraddled out financially. He's made every dollar that belongs to him git to work and do more 'n any dollar ought to do. He's a reacher. Been a-reachin' out and a-reachin' out till it looks like his arm must 'a' got stretched. Owns stock in the railroad—not a majority, but consid'able. Gits control by proxies. Then along come this Diversity Hardwood Company, and he must git his hands on to it. He's got some money, but 'tain't enough. So he puts up his railroad stock for collateral and buys a block of Diversity Company. Then he talks the stockholders into thinkin' he's consid'able big punkin. Two fellers in Grand Rapids that owns control up and makes him president and general manager of the outfit—and takes over his notes and collateral for him. They're a-carryin' him, 'cause they figgered he was a man could make money for 'em. Got that all down, eh?"

"Yes."

"Know what to do with it?"

"No."

"Then p'int your ears and listen."

While Tiffany jogged along at the breakneck pace Zaanan attributed to him the old justice instructed Jim.

Eleven stockholders in the Diversity Hardwood Company were present at the meeting, including Zaanan and Jim. Moran was in the chair. He had raised objection when Jim entered, but was referred to the company's stock-book. The meeting was called to order and routine business completed. The election of directors was imminent.

Jim stood up.

"Mister Chairman," he said, "before we start on this election there is a matter I want to lay before the stockholders."

"We have more important business than to listen to you now," snapped Moran.

"The most important business this meeting can attend to is what I have to lay before them."

"Go ahead, go ahead," said a burly, grizzly-haired man who lounged back in his chair smoking a huge and powerful cigar. "What's on your mind?"

"As a stockholder in this company I charge the president with more than one act prejudicial to the interest of the company and with more than one act reflecting on the honor and business integrity of the concern."

Moran leaped to his feet.

"This is the man who hired a gang of toughs to raid our camps and steal our railroad. He's stolen our timber; he's on the verge of bankruptcy—owing us money—and last night he went on to our property and set fire to Crab Creek Trestle. He'll see the inside of jail for that."

"Now, now, Moran, one at a time," said the big man. "You'll get your chance. Go ahead, young fellow. You've made your statements; now back them up—or git."

"First," said Jim, "this company needs the Le Bar tract. Is that not so?"

"You bet we do," said the big man.

"Moran has had a chance to buy—at a reasonable figure—and has refused even to deal. I have an option on that timber. Because I have it, because he is after my scalp, he won't deal. You've tried to buy of Le Bar for half a dozen years. That's charge number one."

"His price was exorbitant. It was a hold-up," Moran shouted.

"You have never asked a price. I have never put a price on the land—to you or to anybody else. Next, he has done all in his power to cripple the Ashe Clothespin Company, which is your most valuable single asset. He's been bought up by the Clothespin Club. First he hired a man to cripple our machinery; another of his men filled our logs with spikes for us to saw into. His railroad has withheld cars for our shipments. These acts he has done as president of this concern. Is it pleasant to you gentlemen that your president, in your own woods, should spike your own logs and ship them to a valuable customer? These things I am in position to prove. He refused to carry out the terms of this company's contract, would not give us logs, so I had to avail myself of the permission of the contract to seize and operate your logging machinery. And, finally, last night, by his orders, property of this company was destroyed by fire. Michael Moran burned Crab Creek Trestle. This I can prove."

"It's an infernal lie!" Moran shouted.

"There, there," said the big man. "If Mr. Ashe is lying we'll see you have satisfaction. Just prove the burning of the trestle; well let the other matters go for another day."

Zaanan went to the door and called. Steve Gilders came in, rifle under his arm, pushing another individual before him.

"Here's your proof," said Zaanan, dryly. "Go ahead, Steve."

"This here feller," said Steve, "burned the trestle last night. Soaked her with oil and touched her off. Then he took a shot at Mr. Ashe there—and thought he'd got him. Calc'late he thought so till this minnit, for he hain't heard nothin' to the contrary. Now, Kowterski, I seen you. Who told you to burn that there trestle?"

"He did," said Kowterski, pointing to Moran.

Moran sprang toward Kowterski, but Gilders shifted his rifle. "Don't go prancin' round. I guess you know I wouldn't grieve none if I was forced to hurt you, Moran."

"Moran," said the big man, "this isn't altogether unexpected. My good friend, Judge Frame, has been in touch with me, and we've done a bit of investigating ourselves. Now I'll tell you what we're going to do, Wilkins and I. We've held you up; you had us on the blind side. Personally I don't like to be fooled. It r'iles me, and I'm good and plenty r'iled. We sha'n't press the incendiarism charge. Putting you in prison wouldn't make me any happier; but busting you would. This locality won't be broken-hearted to see you removed from it. Your notes are due; we shall not renew. Our attorneys have been notified to take the usual steps to realize on your collateral. Now if I were you I'd clear out. We haven't any more use for you here."

Moran protested, threatened, raved. When he was done and the room was rid of him, the big man turned to Jim:

"I hear you've earned a name, young man. Sudden Jim, is it? A good name, and your father'll be glad to hear of it. Maybe I can give you a piece of news. Saw Welliver and Jenkins yesterday. They're through. The Clothespin Club will be good if you'll cry quits. Meeting next week in Grand Rapids, and you'd better go."

"About that option of yours, son," said the stockholder named Wilkins, "we know what it cost you. You're entitled to your profit. Will two dollars an acre satisfy you? If it will the board, when it is elected, will instruct the treasurer to give you his check for the amount."

The movement of affairs had been too swift even for Sudden Jim. The revolution in his condition had been too rapid. He could scarcely grasp it. Moran done for, himself offered a profit on his option which would pay the note presented that day and leave a pleasant margin of cash! His acceptance was prompt.

He drove back to Diversity with Zaanan after the meeting. For most of the way he was silent, dazed at the outcome of affairs. At last he spoke.

"Judge," said he, "I said you were a great man this afternoon—"

"That's all right, Jim."

"If it hadn't been for you—"

"To be sure! To be sure! It's my business to meddle. And, besides, Clothespin Jimmy and I was raised side by side. He licked me four times 'fore I was twelve year old. He told me to sorter look after you a mite, figgerin' you might need it. And say, son, if I was you I'd go hell-for-leather out to Steve's place. You've been messin' up things with that girl out there. I dun'no' but you ought to git thrashed for actin' so; but you're young and sudden." Zaanan smiled dryly. "'Twa'n't Marie told Moran you was goin' to swoop down on his camp; it was that young Newell up to your office. Call to mind, it was him warned you the trestle was goin' to burn. Moran's had him bought up quite a spell."

"Judge—" said Jim. "Judge—"

"Yes, son, you're as big a dum fool as you figger you are, and maybe more. The young is inclined to value themselves high."

"Will you drive me out to her? Now? She'll never forget—never forgive—what I said to her and believed; but I've got to tell her. I've got to beg her forgiveness."

"While you're doin' your beggin'," said Zaanan, shrewdly, "you might throw in a few words about how much you think of her. Eh? That kind of talk is sort of flavorin' in a girl's ear."

"There is a good deal of it for me to say," said Jim.

He did not speak again until the miles to Steve Gilders's shanty were traversed, until they stood at the low door of the house. Jim rushed ahead of Zaanan, opened the door.

"Is she—Where is she? Can I—I must see her now!" he said to the astonished woman who had sat with Marie through the night.

"She's perked up a mite," said the woman, "but she don't act like she was happy. Go right in. She's able to talk to folks now."

Jim opened the door and entered the bedroom softly. He found Marie's eyes on his face as he turned toward the bed, dark wells of misery.

"Marie," he whispered, and knelt by her side, his hand fumbling for her hand. "Marie, it was cruel. I—I have no excuse to offer you. Where I should have trusted I failed to trust. I loved you—but I was not worthy to love you. Even when I believed you had done that thing, I loved you. I could not tear it out of my heart. There is nothing I can do but tell you how my love failed, and beg you to forgive me if you can. What is gone is gone. I have lost you, and I know the bitterness of loss."

She turned her face toward him; her eyes were beautiful—softly, tenderly beautiful.

"I—am not lost," she whispered, "so—so badly that you can't find me—if you look."

"Marie!"

"Jim, last night I learned something about love. I know what it is. I knew you would learn the truth. All that—I put aside. While I was trying to reach you I put it aside. I knew love would abide, through griefs, through whatever had gone before, whatever was to come. I loved you—would always love you. Do you know, Jim, I had made up my mind to fight for my love? Yes, if others had not proved I did not do that thing, I should have proved it to you myself. Because I—wanted you, Jim. Because I had to have you."

He clung to her hand, speechless. A ray of glory had fallen upon him, and he was blinded with it.

"Jim," she said, "you have never kissed me. You aren't acting like—the Sudden Jim I want for my own."